More praise for *Dibs: A Train of Thought*

Clint McCown's original and magnificent *Dibs* explores how "the mind expands / from what to why," while adding a deftly quiet drama, for McCown is a kind of poetic "hoarder" countering the way the world is "always / falling / away from us." With an engaging conversational style along a narrow "train of thought," *Dibs* carries us through science and cosmology, the nature of language and metaphor, dream and reality, and from trailer parks to East Germany, Hamlet to Buddhism, and so much more, all the time worrying about everyday issues such as the right tape to fix plumbing. It is his voice, and an impeccable sense of the short line that engages us as if we were sitting across the table in a pub, calling out "dibs" on some subject, sometimes revealing autobiographical details, always weaving in a stream of conscious manner, and yet always hoping for a "unified theory / of everything." As he tells us at one point, "starting anywhere / you can go / anywhere," and we do, to a whole new vison of what poetry can do.

—Richard Jackson, author of *Footprints* and *The Heart as Framed: New and Select Poems*

Other books by Clint McCown

Poems

Labyrinthiad
Sidetracks
Wind Over Water
Dead Languages
Total Balance Farm
The Dictionary of Unspellable Noises:
New & Selected Poems, 1975-2018

Fiction

The Member-Guest
War Memorials
The Weatherman
Haints
Music for Hard Times:
New and Selected Stories

Craft

Mr. Potato Head vs. Freud:
Lessons on the Craft of Writing Fiction

Essays

Son of the Secret Service

DIBS

A TRAIN OF THOUGHT

Clint McCown

Press 53
Winston-Salem

Press 53, LLC
PO Box 30314
Winston-Salem, NC 27130

First Edition

Cover design by Kevin Morgan Watson

Library of Congress Control Number
2026934857

ISBN 978-1-968783-03-7

for Archie Ammons,
a friend lost in the first act;
for Keith Ratzlaff and Jeff Gundy,
friends found in the second,
and Dawn Cooper McCown
who makes sense of the third

Thinking is the best way
to travel —

The Moody Blues

DIBS

Dibs
    on this train
    starting nowhere

(as *starting*
    forges moments
    bringing thought;
and *nowhere*
    is an honest place,
    absent the
    bias of being)

    caught now,
    this train,
    this moment,
in the act
    of becoming.
We're free
        to move
    where movement
        takes us.

Well,
maybe not entirely
free:
all undertakings
call for
boundaries,
or else they'll
dissipate in
aimless
wandering
(a dog
let off the leash,
soon lost,
no words
to bring it back
from its digressions),

and trains of thought
are no exception;
here
we're
bound by shape
(a narrow track
for focus)
and by direction
(of a rolling movement
toward).

Toward what? I ask
on your behalf
and mine.

But I don't know:
my wisdom jar
is empty.

Still, hopes are high
(endemic to
beginners
in their first

unsteady steps) —
no goal in mind,
no scaffolding
of doctrine
to restrain
the coming text;
the only plan:
to follow
inclinations
as they rise —
with faith
that every start
implies
arrival
somewhere
further down the line;

with maybe something
unforeseen
unspooling
between the brackets:
a dusty trunk
brought down
from the attic,
photo albums
left unlooked at
for a while;
images
of light, maybe,
strobing past a window;
a window,
maybe,
framing glints of light.

I'm thinking now
photography
is proof
that any image
can be
tangible,

hijacked
          from its moment,
each moment
          a boxcar,
          each boxcar
          a holder of
                    souvenirs,
          each souvenir,
                    a boxcar
                    of its own.

That's how
          memory works.
What lies
          behind us
          pushes
          us ahead,
as time's momentum
                    builds.
The ticket
          for this trip
is already
in your pocket,
                    paid for
                    by all
the dazzling and
dark discoveries
          it took
          to get this far.
We've all
          brought baggage

          to this train.

The greatest hope
          is for a track
          that takes us
somewhere different
from the everywhere
          we've been.

What I mean is:
bridges
          should be crossed;
and you and I
should come to
          see ourselves
          through lenses
of a different grind.

Each window here
          might also
          be a mirror
                    of a kind —
as writing serves as
          self-reflection
          once removed,
writer facing reader,
reader facing writer
          facing self.
          Good luck to us,
          in that regard.

I'm halfway qualified
          for this.
My mind can still
          catch its breath
                    on the moon,
          but better when
the moon is full;
          if just
          a cutting edge,
I tend towards
          speechlessness.

Full moons get
the best publicity.
          That's natural:
a slivered moon
          won't amplify
the howls of

any wolf or
grandstand drunk.
No separated lovers
stare
forlornly
at a slim hangnail
of reflected light.
(Not in poems,
anyway;
in the real world
anything goes —
a dark moon
might be preferable
on prom night
in the back seat of
someone's Chrysler)

But while we're
looking outward
at the night sky,
let me say
the body is
a kind of
space suit
keeping us together
until the slingshot
of earth's gravity
sends us
on our way again.
In it,
we cry for losses
yet to come,
forget
whatever
blessed us here.

The literal is easy:
we're mainly built
from half a dozen
elements,

common as dirt,
        with five more
        adding
        a pound or two.
But after that,
a trace of
        minor elements
        is all it takes
        to keep
        the party going,
some with names
        you might not
        even know
(molybdenum, anyone?)
Science says
they're indispensable
        to life.

So here we are,
        a layered
                thickening
in the atmosphere
        endowed with
        basics
        of perception:
eyes adjusted to a
narrow spectrum,
        ears tuned to a
        limited range
(though hearing can be
        problematic:
science ties it
to the
        motion of a wave,
        but
if words appear
        on a
        page
—these words,
for example,

            on this page—
do they make a sound
            in the mind?
For me, they do.
But that's imaginary,
            no wave in sight.
            What are we
supposed
to make of that?),
a nose too weak to
            track down prey
            unless we're
            in the parking lot
            of a rib joint,
a tongue of
            unsophisticated
            tastes
(sour, bitter, salty, sweet—
plus savory
            to tell
            the brain
            where protein is),
and last of all
a tactile sense
            to tell us
            mud is soft,
            cold days
                        are cold,
            and pain
                        awaits us
                        at the bottom
                        of a fall.

Still, we work
with what we have,
            hacking our way
            forward
through whatever jungle
            dares to
            slow us down.

It's the open field
we crave,
one that shows
the fullness
of the empty sky.

We hope there will be
starlight, always,
and maybe always
hope,
and maybe
all the maybes
will deliver in the end.

I know: hope
is a
scarecrow
in a hard wind,
frail before
the ravenous.
And maybe
it's the
saddest thing
of all.

But
maybe this time

crows will
scatter
to the trees,
while new growth
rises.
Let's
hope so
anyway.

That's what
keeps us going,
after all:

              this blind maybe,
              this saddest thing.

But why come along
              with me
              at all?
What do I know?
Nothing much,
              though it takes
a lot of will power
              not to pretend
              to know things
(see: politics,
              religion,
              other forms
              of war).
But I can't even
              tell you
where the sky begins,
              though it's
              right there,
possibly within
                            my reach.

A single person
                            thinking,
              that's all
              this is —
                            a search
                            for signs
suggesting whether
              one thought
              leads to many
or the first thought
              holds them all:
the world as
              difference
                            or
              a form of unity.

Which is it?
Something I say here
could be
          deeply,
          cosmically
          right,
but if so,
          it might
          just be
          a lucky guess.

Still, a lot of
          good things
got built on
          lucky guesses,
          so I'll
          shrug my way
                    onward.
I can at least
          claim to know
what it's like

          to step off
          a cliff
          I didn't know
          was there
(the Tim's Ford
overlook, 1987)

          the feeling
          of finite
          uncertainty

          in a drop
          that
          may,
          in terms of
          life
          or
          death,

be
bottomless;

And in that fall
I faced
the knowledge
that I may
have made
my last mistake;

that time
could not
turn back
to offer me
salvation,

even for a
microsecond,

and whatever
blunt physics
I had
blundered into

would be
inescapable.

But

at the
bottom
of that
fraction
of my plummet
flashed a glimmer
of a chance —

that the depth
might not

                    be
                    deadly,

that I might catch
          a steep angle
                    of grace
and roll with it
                    down a
          half-forgiving
          slope.

Hope
          is what it was.
          And it was
                    right.

To clarify a point:
          Hoping is not
          a form of wishing,
but a form of trust
          (that every future
                    holds
                    a capability
          to bypass
whatever trouble
          might be
          on the way,
          that the universe
                    might,
                    in any
                    given case,
          shield us from
the light that burns,
the dark that freezes,
the wind
          that overcomes;
even from the sword
          that dangles.
And sometimes
                    it does).

A wish,
meanwhile,
is often
a complaint,
a blatant *ask*
for things
to be different,
a *want*
often greedy
and
tinged with regret.

We can wish
to change the past,
but we know better
than to hope for it.
The horse that lost
will always lose,
the winner
always will have won.

Fear, I fear,
is the progenitor
of hope,
and I have many fears
to hope against—
the worst might be
that our
sad brand
of progress
takes us nowhere
but the precipice;
that lemmings
are the image of
ourselves.
I also fear
that's not a fear at all,
but simple
recognition.

I wish it could be
otherwise.

Many of us
heard a song
when we were
young
that started
When you wish
upon a star
makes no difference
who you are
and that much is true.
But
the nearest star
is Proxima Centauri
at 4.24 light years away,
and even if
it has
nothing better
to do
than help you win
the lottery,
by the time
it gets your
message
and moves heaven
a little
to the left
to make it all
work out,
you'll be
either dust
or ash,
along with
everybody else.

Maybe wishing is
just one more
strictly human

trait.
And who could
blame us
for maintaining
such a
hopelessly
hopeful
indulgence
across our millennia?
For well or ill,
we all
probably get
what we deserve,
and who can live
comfortably
with that?

But here's a piece of
country wisdom
given to me
ages ago
by my
cousin Doug:

Wish in one hand,
shit in the other;
see which
fills up first.

I hope
nobody
finds that
offensive.

A wish can be wistful,
lighter than air,
which separates it from
longing,
that bag of bricks

we tote
without end.

Naturally, we want
to fix the world,
but the place
is just too big for that.
The best we can
hope for
is to improve
whatever
over-crowded
ledge
we're balanced on.

I write,
but that's
of little use.
The guy who
replaces
brake pads
at the tire store
does more real-world
good
for the community.
The best I have
to offer
is a close-up look
at something
other than
yourself,
which might,
upon reflection,
show you
something you can use.
You might stand
a few extra
seconds
at the morning mirror
and wonder

what's there.
But I can't save you
from
blowing through
a stop sign.

I can tell you this
about myself:
I share
the toddler's joy
standing
in the rain
in summertime;
but I also know
the caveman's
simple satisfaction
of sitting sheltered
from the storm.
One primal hope
is to be safe
from the lightning.

Another thing
I can tell you
about myself:
when I was young
I took a
state-created
personality exam
that told me
I was not
cut out for jail.
But who is?
And who can avoid
going there?
We're stuck
with school,
with work,
with regimented play,
and in the end,

most likely,
        a hospital
        or care facility,
each of which
        confines us
to a schedule,
        a uniform,
        a standard
                of behavior.
Even the lone hunter
        in the woods
        is bound by
        protocols and
                seasons.
Prison, it seems,
                sums up
                the basics
                of society;
if you can
make it there,
        you can make it
                anywhere.

        I guess that’s
        how I once
        wound up
        living
        on the street;
and why
        I didn’t
                stay there.

As I’m dyslexic now
        (by-product
        of disruptions
        in my brain)
watch out for
                odd
                reversals
here and there.

When I say *dog*
I might mean
god
(which could make
sense,
with *deified*
a palindrome).

And let me
level
with you further:
being taught well
(I was)
is not the same as
learning well—
it took me years
to realize
a supermarket cake
looks better
than it tastes—
so I can't
guarantee
results.

The motto on my
Scottish family crest
is
If I Can,
which stakes a claim
on failure
from the start.
And yet
the sacred animal
of Scotland
is the
unicorn,
which reassures me.

Sometimes you might
think

I repeat
myself,
but that's impossible.
Words can't
enter
the same world
twice.
I repeat:
words can't
enter
the same world
twice,
and in the space
between
what was said
and what was said
again,
a thousand people
died,
a thousand and five
were born,
billions of emotions
shifted,
opinions changed,
guns discharged,
a tree
fell in the forest
and brought
forth
good vibrations,
and many someones
turned on
many radios
and heard
The Beach Boys.
And you, too,
changed,
entered
the second phrase
with different

expectations,
a fresh
heartbeat,
and a shorter life.

Since we're in motion
now,
I'm not sure
I can tell you
who I am,
only
how fast
I'm changing
(Heisenberg, et cetera):
in one
now-frozen frame
I'm a ten-year-old boy
given a ladder and
a broad bristle brush
by my father
and told
to paint the lower side
of the house,
which I did,
coating the
cinder blocks and
corrugated shingles
with a tan color
I disliked.
Eventually a spread
of pyracantha
climbed the wall,
lovely
in its
firethorn way,
negating the
unsightliness
it clung to.

That side yard
was always damp,
a little mossy,
from an underground
spring
and my father cut a
willow branch
from the tree
out front
and stuck it
in the center
of the unseeable flow.
That stick took root
and flourished
at a rate
uncanny,
outlasting
its source,
its first identity,
which had to be
cut down
when
too-aggressive
roots
crept into
the sewer line.

Idyllic days, I guess,
since that's
what childhood is
supposed to be
when looked at
from the safe haven
of a future self,

although I do recall
an older
boy
who lurked next door—
Larry—

wiry and mean,
        who shot the leg
        off my cat
and slept
        on a pool table
and
who used to hurl me
        with vicious glee
        on the long
        rope swing
that hung from the
        dead
        hackberry
between our houses,
not out and back,
        like you see
        in old movies
with carefree kids,
but round and round
        the hollowed
                trunk,
like tetherball,
        until my body
        wrapped itself
to the rough bark
        and I fell
        into the dirt,
        scraped
                and bruised.
Larry liked the terror
        he imagined
        he invoked,
but
        secretly
        I craved
that sense of
        flying,
my thin frame stretched
        parallel
        to the earth,

the pull of my weight
against the
          knotted
                    hemp,
the danger of letting go
          balanced
against the
          certainty of
          a hard end
                    if I didn't.

There's payment owed
          for almost
          every pleasure,
          every love.
The sunniest of days
requires a slathering;
the green pond
          invites a swim
          but there are leeches;
the cooling dark of a
          child's
          summer night
fans an inborn fear
          of something
rank and unstoppable
          hiding
          in the gloom,
                    waiting.

We're all made strange
          by experience,
because experience
          is whatever
          comes to us
                    new:
          the first sense
          of hunger,
          the first bounce
                    of a ball,

the first seeing
of the world
beyond
the wall;
the first flutter
in the heart,
the first shock
of pain,
the first
disappointment,
the first tears.

I have slept on a bed
of cold granite
and in a bed of fire;
I have slept
beneath
a canopy of
leaves
and
beneath
a gold
chandelier.
I have slept in class
and in cars
and on trains.
I have slept
in noisy
bleachers
at the game.
I have slept
hooked to
machines.
I have slept
in doorways.
I have slept
on the water.
I have slept in the sky.

What ancestor
        would believe
        our ordinary lives;
could
comprehend
        the miracle
of dozing off
        at nearly
                the speed
                of sound?

We inherit traits,
        but not
        experience:
I have used
        an outhouse,
        but not
as a way of life.
        I have
chopped wood,
but not
        to survive.
        I have boiled
        water
        for drink,
                but not
as a necessary routine.
I have not
        been bled
        by doctors,
crossed the prairies
        or the deserts
        by wagon,
or died
for want of aspirin
to bring a fever down.

Nevertheless
        (a lovely
        word to carve

into a castle wall),
like you, I bring
experience
of my own,
to every new
experience
that comes along,
this
being one
of them.

In short:
the here-and-now
lays claim
to what I'm up to,
and
I do think
intentionality
is owed.

One early hope
is that I
sidestep
emptiness—
those lost stretches
on a long
ride
known only
by the pivot back:
What landscape
did I just
pass through?

Moreover (fine word
of its own,
a form
of linkage,
coupling one thought
to another),
if I can

I'll keep away from
nonsense:
no blue monkeys
singing medleys of
medieval sadnesses
or tapping out
dance rhythms
on the rings
of Saturn,
or whatever:
Crap like that can
kill a poem
(if that's
what this thing
is).
I've seen enough
cheap hokum
in my day.
If you don't get
what I'm getting at,
that's on me.

And furthermore (a
scornful,
lecturing
word, too uppity
at times):
there'll be no
wine-dark surfaces
passed off
as unplumbed depth,
so don't mistake
some grease spot
on a rag
as shorthand
for apocalypse.

No fake profound,
is what I mean,
so if you read

The day was
taller than
a ladder in
an unseen room,
know that some typesetter
has run amuck
or
I've had another stroke.

One thing I'd like
to do here
is be myself,
but that's a magic act
few can
muster.
We all put effort
into costume design:
maybe you taught yourself
to be funny
to avoid the terror
of being laughed at,
or so people
wouldn't see
the ill-formed
lump of clay
the mirror
said you were;
maybe you
raised your hand
in class so you
could be an island
with a rocky shore;
maybe you sat
quiet and still
so people would
mistake you
for a coat
at the bottom
of the pile.
The dread of course

is that the final
nesting doll
will turn out empty,
so we leave it
on the shelf.

What I mean is,
I'll be open
with you
if I can,
but expect
mixed results.
Writing
is a display window
in a department store,
and the items
you see there
are meant to
draw you in.
Not a con, exactly.
You might pick up
a bargain.

Feel free to think—
if something here
provokes it;
but don't get
sidetracked
into second-guessing
what I
might have meant.
This isn't English class.

And to that point:
I'll leave all
red wheelbarrows
by the door;
not much depends
upon them
anymore.

And though I come
from Tennessee,
I'll place no jars
upon a hill
just to point out how
un-bushlike,
un-bearlike
they are.
What's obvious is
obvious,
so
let's cut to the chase:

I've heard that beauty
is the thing,
but I'm contrarian
in that regard.
Apologies to Keats,
but
he was wrong
about the
shared identity
all beauty
holds with truth.
The coral snake
has
splendored rings,
but truth
is in the strike.
Violence
is never pretty
but
we shouldn't
look away,
lest it turn
in our direction.
(p.s. don't trust
anyone
who trains a dog
to harm;

likewise,
anyone
who trains a god
to harm.)

The scarlet king snake,
almost
the mirror image
of the coral,
wouldn't harm
a child;
it's power is
immunity
to venom —
plus a knack
for constriction —
and it eats
the deadly coral
after squeezing out
the life.

Of course,
we could kill
either one.
Rock, paper, scissors:
that's the balance
of nature.

What I mean is:
truth,
is the bigger
toolbox —
not that I have
any better grip
on its slick handle
than you,
just that I'd rather
stare
at an unsolved
equation

on a chalkboard
than a catalogue
of paint splotches.
In short, I won't
be pointing out
petunias
without good reason,
and any rose that
shows its
barb-sheltered
face
will likely be rooted
in manure.

Not that I'm down
on beauty,
per se.
I flushed a bluebird
from a bush
by the porch
yesterday
and watched it flit
across the gravel drive
and rise into
the deepening woods.
I felt the beauty
in its flight.
But later on
I saw a hawk
gliding low
through that
same stand of trees,
silent,
angling
without effort,
blending in,
and felt
the certainty
of power.
Not just beauty:

something
stronger.

One problem
is the cryptic:
pure abstractions
might sound
weighty
but
they
won't
save
the canary.

Please note
there will be
metaphors
along our route,
(see above)
the *lingua franca*
on this train,
(which is itself a
metaphor,
self-conscious
as all get-out);
the world is just
a classroom,
after all,
that teaches us
about
itself;
and everything is
allegory there
as well as here —
the turning leaf,
the drop of rain,
the yellow
flower
pushing through
the sidewalk crack.

Also, watch for
vast complexities
reduced
to simple
observations,
as I am wont to do,
mostly in iambic form.
I'm sorry for the
stiltedness
of that.

But maybe poems
are always posed —
tuxedoed
constructs
leaning
nonchalantly
on the champagne bar,
straining
to look natural.
It's a hard sell,
believe you me,
and sometimes
even nature
burps at the opera.

In poetry,
that perfect leaf
on that prefect branch
is perfect only in
the way we frame it.
In truth,
it's just a leaf
on a branch —
which ought to be
miracle enough
for anybody.
Perfection goes
without saying;
mere existence

          covers that base
          nicely.

Sure,
beauty is a
          sometime
                    byproduct
          in the natural realm
          but so are
                    the ugly
                    and
                    the weird.
When a lady mantis
          bites the head off
          her mate,
it's not to insure fidelity.
Note, too,
   the dodo,
          the lemming,
the duckbill platypus.
Penguins in the jungle,
          for god's sake
          (look it up).
   The tiny desert
                    rain frog
          of South Africa,
so unsightly
it's cute
          and squeaks
          like a dog toy.
So who's to say
          what's natural
          or right?

Perfect
          is a fabrication
          we employ
          to shore up our
aesthetic preferences.
Applying it

self-consciously
to the
natural world
is redundant.
Believe in the perfect
as something
set
apart,
and reality
becomes
unnatural.

That's one connection
you and I
can share:
we're both living
the same
unnatural story,
hazarding best guesses
to get us
through the day.
We might have
some idea
of where we want
to go,
but not which road
will get us there.
Sometimes, when a
midnight wind
rattles
the shutters,
we aren't entirely sure
the place
we're longing for
is real.

I saw the bluebird again
this morning,
early, when
the mist still hugged

the hilltops.
It swooped down
this time
from the high
wooded edge
to that same bush
near the house,
straight across my path.
I could almost
have reached out and
touched it;
got the same glad
feeling as before
from that
unlooked for
flicker of beauty.
But later,
mid-afternoon,
I opened up a box
of books
I'd stored too near the
garage door,
and found that seepage
ruined
eighteen
precious
volumes
signed and gifted
from old friends,
some of them
dead now.
The outcome:
a new appreciation for
what survives,
fresh longings
for what was lost.
But I guess
we never know
what's coming.
Often

I don't know
what's already
here.

In the early hours
I open my eyes
to a bombardment
of questions and
answers
(unequal in proportion)
and my body
says
Go back to sleep
but
my mind says
Take care of this mess,
and it's like
my motorcycle days
when
I'd dip into a
deep
depression
on a country road,
a hollow
along a creek bed,
say,
and the dank
dark air
would drop into a
sudden chill,
and lying there
in the warm bed
my insides
sink
and I think
No,
there's nothing real
to worry about,
though of course
there always is

if worry
is the choice
        you want to make.
        So usually
I get up and
do something
        solid enough
        to hang an
        expectation on:
making coffee,
feeding the animals,
turning on lights.

Abstractions can be
        useful,
        if there's nothing
that needs hammering;
they earn their keep
        by naming
the invisible,
                containing
        the ineffable:
                (love
                hate
        happiness
        despair
        truth & beauty
and the like)
but travel needs
        a vehicle
        of substance,
so
matter is
what's called for here
        (both definitions
        work).

Let's start with
        limestone,
        sand, and

soda crystals,
blended to a
balance
that produces glass
(can be seen through,
can reflect,
same as water,
same as memory).

Add warp to cure
the eye's
distortions
and a tint
of metal oxide
(keeps the sun at bay)
and just like that
we're on our way
to
making spectacles
(archaic word,
connecting
both ends
of vision — through
spectacles
we see
spectacles).

The mind's eye, I'll say,
is more nearsighted
than far,
especially in
remembrance,
but time adjusts
our vision,
turning
old pains laughable,
old gripes
toothless.

But looking back
in idle reminiscence
has a cost:
In time
we undestand
the only sin
we can't atone for
is wasting time.

So dump all grudges at
the junk yard or
the dump.
The only souvenirs
you'll need
are ones you'll
cry for losing.

But everything's
a souvenir,
I guess.
Not just the
ticket stub
to the Cub's game
where you saw
Sammy Sosa
hit two home runs,
or that musty
Broadway play bill
for
Phantom of the Opera,
but all
the rest of it, too:
every book
and china cup,
the socks
in your
sock drawer,
the wrapped bar
of guest soap
grown dingy

in the cabinet,
and music,
and friendships,
and longings,
and disappointments,
and every memory that
mindlessly persists.
The world is always
falling
away
from
us.
It's no wonder we
cling tight
to what we can.

Some scenes
survive illogically—
old fragments
flitting
through the mind,
outtakes
of a plotless
silent film:

The Florida gulf,
that day
of digging
on the beach
when I was three,
white sand
warming my toes,
the tiny red shovel,
the cracked
blue bucket,
the wind
speaking strangely
in my ear,
the water
lapping in and out,

a treasure
of pink shells,
the flat horizon
stretching past
what I could
know,
blurred misgivings
as my mother
waded out
into the roiling surf.

That moment came
unbidden.
It happens to be
mine alone,
all other figures
from that day—
parents,
uncles,
aunts—
now drawn away
by
the usual tide.

No doubt
you have your own
version
of that scene,
maybe not
at the beach
but in a
mountain
meadow
or a shoe store
in the city
or
on the pebbled lot
where you first
played on the
monkey bars,

or by the lily pond
        in your
        grandmother's
                side yard;
        your first entry
        into
        your first school,
        or church
        or
        department store.
It could be anything,
        is what I'm saying,
and for you it has
        a special value
        you don't fully
                understand,
        a value linked
        to feelings
for which you've
not yet learned
                the words.

Or maybe there
        are no words.

Some memories,
        of course,
are knapsacks
        stuffed with
        roofing nails
that dig into
                your spine
        with every
        forward step:
betrayals
        and lost loves,
for example,
        or deaths
        from which
        no preparation

saves us
(parents, children,
any spirit
kindred to your own).
It takes a
telescope
to bring those galaxies
in focus.

Not that I would
have the past
be anything
but what it was:
tragedy
is too important
to be tampered with—
a fulcrum
bringing change;
even in the aftermath
of dire calamity,
grant me
three wishes
and they would grow
dusty
on the shelf.

So let's set aside
the past
for now,
and trust
that it will reassert itself
when past
fits present need.

If all goes well,
each tick
along this track will
take us somewhere
yet unseen,
the map unfolding

randomly before us;
with luck,
we'll offload freight
from every boxcar
we can't help
but drag behind —
the raw tonnage
of regrets
and guilts
and weaknesses.
That's what we are,
in part:
containers of
whatever wounds the
earth delivered unto us,
the friction building
till we finally derail;

or maybe
not derail, but
save ourselves
by catching on,
by welcoming
some new epiphany:
momentum brings
momentum brings
momentum
and we shed
dead weight,
the act of thinking
lightens us,
our spirit
thinning
into whistling air
and
merging into
winds
that stabilize
our travel on the track.

Imagine twin rails
gleaming
as they narrow
toward a distant graph
of peaks:
now here
we go,
(so close, I notice, to
nowhere
we go)
barreling along
the
straightaway
then curling through
a range
of cursive curves
riding the
ridge lines
down-hilling
the hollows
into deepening
dales
then
banking
hard,
without warning
without punctuation
through harrowing
marsh-side bends
almost tipping
almost
plunging to an
inky sea
of suffocating reeds
all in the name of
overcoming limitations.

Sounds dangerous,
but no.
Imagination

has its limits,
and harm is one of them.
This ride will be
unburdening:
no dire
destructions,
no untoward
consequence;
no tragic tumbling,
no terrified
engulfment
as the quicksand
closes overhead,
no futile thrashing
in some swampy
byway bog
as outstretched fingers
grasp
one final handful
of empty air
and then go under.

Instead:
the ground beneath us
will continue,
firm,
always steady rails
to set this thing upon,
to keep us
moving forward,
all aboard.

Or has language
pulled the rug
already?
Is saying we won't
say a thing
just
letting the cold, cold
mirror

say it
for us?

No easy passage, then.
You've been outside,
you've seen the news:
the world is
always up to something,
and travel
punishes
the body:
the running tumble,
jetlag,
even
brain fatigue from
thinking
thinking
thinking
so here and there
a cloud or two
will likely darken
into storm,
the meadows quake,
the waters rise,
the gales tear loose
all forms of
opposition.

Gas-pump canopies,
too tall to offer shelter
from the rain,
might topple to their
concrete beds,
while five-board fences
snap and rise.
Green gardens,
newly trimmed,
might spiral
into shreds,
release their gnomes

and plastic chairs
skyward
to the
deafening air.
Tin run-in sheds
might blithely tumble
into mobile homes,
and billboards
advertising
all our best
might cleave
and cleave again
into
a
thousand
daggered
wings.
Yes, a good vortex
can splinter anything—
especially
in metaphor—
though
in most cases
like adheres
to like
even in bad weather.
A vein of gold,
of iron,
of silver
snakes
through the earth as
a bound community
of atoms,
no strays breaking off
to go exploring,
each iota's
primal nature
to remain subsumed
among identical
manifestations

of itself,
its world
an unbroken mirror.
Even wind moves
in its own channel.
The outer layer
of any structure,
molecular or otherwise,
from the dust-bunnies
on the floor
to the dust-ball
that is our
planet,
clings fast
to its own
edge,
one side embracing
like,
the other
confronting alien form,
an otherness,
or maybe
nothingness,
with nothing
but the thin
defining strain
of
surface tension
holding the collective
together,
even in a bead
of water,
even in a galaxy
of stars,
even in
tribes of
humanity who learned
early
the dangers
of going it alone

against whatever
                hunger
        waited in the night.

We sit
        facing the fire,
        facing one another
                across the fire,
watching past each other
        through the fire,
ready to give warning
        when that thing
        from the darkness
                finally
                dares
                its approach.

Is fear of isolation
(or
        the need not to be
        isolated)
        the glue
        that binds
the infinite components
of the tangible?
Some religions preach
                separation
                from God
as the ultimate
                punishment,
and maybe that's true
        all the way down
        to the
        hydrogen atom.
Nothing wants to be
                cast adrift.
That's chaos:
        no form,
        no direction,
        no unities

of purpose;
existence in a
non-constructed
form,
the universe reduced to
a confetti of atoms
blizzarding
through space.

But
I remain determined
not
to let that happen here.
Or at least
I'll draw the line
on total
catastrophic
entropy.
We might
need just a bit
of trouble
here and there.
Who'd want a life
without the joy
of overcoming strife?
Sun is the
light-giver,
and we all know
how important
that is;
but clouds protect us
from the burn.
Night is
the earth's
own shadow,
and though
at times we
fear
the dark,
it ultimately saves us.

The versions
of paradise
I've heard
are stultifying.
Who cares
what the streets are
paved with?
Harp music
is lovely
but heaven needs
to be more
than an eternal
elevator ride.
In the end,
which is what
we're talking about,
I'm not one for
lounging
on a beach chair.

Explore all options,
is what I'm saying.

A city walk is just
an exercise
in artifice;
the country is a
better proving ground.
A peat bog
will show you
who
and what
you are:
mostly water, but
otherwise
compacted
layers
of preserved decay,
marked by
occasional patches

of superficial growth;
takes a firm hold of
whatever
comes its way.

We have no peat bogs
in my neighborhood,
but we have
other things:
yesterday
the electric gate
shorted out
so I lifted
the terra cotta pot
I use
to house
the battery
and found a
six-foot blacksnake
knotted on
the terminals.
It took a few pokes to
get him moving,
like me in
7th grade
when I had to
get up for
school.
I'm fond of blacksnakes —
harmeless
but to vermin —
though if I had
my druthers,
we'd have a
king snake
in the yard
to keep
the copperheads
at bay.
We all could use

a good king snake
now and again.

But I'd like this train
to offer more
expansive sights:
My hope (that
word again)
is that whatever
shapeless thing
the heart pines for
will carve itself
across the rocky crags
of a cliff face,
easy to read.
But even then
lightning
could reap
the tallest trees, and
every vein of ore
could cough up
rust.
Failure always lurks,
is what I mean.

Sure, thinking is where
answers lie,
but not all thoughts
arrive
unscathed.
That single ragged shoe
you saw
in the gutter
on your way
to work
spells tragedy minus
the details.
Just pay attention,
and the mysteries
will multiply.

Dibs
on those, as well.
Especially those,
however fleeting
or misleadingly
mundane.
Each landscape
is the mirror
of our needs,
though
what we see
is always less
than what
we think
we want.

Dibs on the scrapheap
where nothing
falls short of
expectations

on colors not included
in the crayon box

on peripheral vision,
begetter
of ghosts

on unfounded optimism
where the
dark moon,
we claim,
is new

on thinking every sky
a fingerprint

on what separates
the shrill shriek
of one animal

from another
when the message
is the same.

on the many meanings
of the sigh

on thorny weeds that
grow from
lost loves

and on that portion of
being
as yet unnamed—

which is most of it.

But calling dibs
is never quite enough,
is it?
I should have
launched all this
in proper form:
an invocation
might have
set things right—
that opening gambit
common
to long poems
and desperate prayer,
a calculated call-out
to some
possibly compliant
haint,
a spirit dogsbody
that might be
hovering
in the neighborhood,
looking for work.

But why create at all?
Well,
time is what
we all run out of,
and life becomes
a game of
find the face
in the picture
before you go.
and the face
could be God
or the mirrored self
or the one true love,
whatever myth
you need
the most.
The problem
with the real world
is that it's
outnumbered
by imaginary ones.
So
we create something—
a Mona Lisa,
a needlepoint seat cover,
a concrete stoop
on the back
of the house,
a game plan
for the masses,
or any other surrogate
of progeny.
Then we can
imagine ourselves
leaving without
really leaving,
which is the root
of all desires.

Art casts that drive
as feminine:
the ninefold muses,
earnest daughters
of Zeus,
each with a gift
but not much
personality;
historically,
a comely gaggle
of alabaster ladies
in sculpted gowns
who stop by
on occasion
on a mission
of support.
Cheerleaders, really.

Without them
we couldn't
slap two hunks
of clay together.
No paint could hit
the canvas,
all notes would be
discordant
as punk rock,
words would clot
inside the quill.
Or so they say.

But what are muses,
anyway?
External entities,
as advertised?
If so,
will they come
when called
like a hungry dog?
Do they have to be

coaxed,
cajoled
bribed
somehow
with arty promises?
Or do they have to be
hunted
tracked
cornered
with a barrage
of words,
some of which
might
hit the mark?
Or are they maybe
a kind of
current
to be
plugged into,
a subsidiary of
the main flow?
Or (here's a
radical departure)
are they an
inborn part
of every self,
something always there,
waiting
to be
invited out?

Calliope would be
the one I'd ask for,
by the way,
the only one who married
and had kids.
She must know just how
tough we have it
down here in the mire.
In verse, she separates

the didn’ts
        from the dids.

But muses
        (regardless of
        the source)
are clueless
                as to how
                to market
        what they muse.
So minor poets
        go unread;
the great ones also
        go unread —
though far more tragically.

And yet
we all persist
        in something
                useless:
        Scrabble,
                golf, TV,
whatever fills
        whatever void
        we’re drifting in.

I’ve got no claim
on Mount Parnassus,
        Helicon,
or any other
        elevated ground.
I’m anchored
        in the floodplain;
my pedigree’s the river,
same as yours.
        Time is
        our current,
and our currency.
        Do something,
says the river,

while you
still can.

Accordingly,
in this dry season
I plant my feet
in the scuffed dirt
beneath the
slatted swing
in my backyard
and give the earth
a shove.
My power over
planetary
movement
should be nil:
And yet it moves.

The bough above me
creaks
in mild complaint,
but summer heat
depletes the life of me;
I need some
semblance of a breeze
to keep me here,
tired passenger,
on yet another
pendulum,
adrift
but baggage free.

I'm sure a cool wind
must be blowing
into being now,
this minute,
somewhere—
the arctic,
the antarctic,
the mountain peak

                        next door —
            but that's no help:
    like you,
            I'm here:
            stuck where I am
in that ongoing
            intersection
        of space and time.
We have to make do,
            even on
            unseasonable days.

The urge to move
        is the ghost
        in every living form,
haunting its host
                        in the flotsam
of each bodily cell.
            We're mostly water,
        after all,
and water turns
            stagnant
            if it stands
            too still.
That's why we're
                        of the river,
                        not the pond.

Nearby
in unmowed grass
            the old dog
is dying,
has been
            for a while now,
            but his tail still
        gives a wag
so we don't intervene.

He's taught me things:
            that eyes

are useless
if the brain is dark;
that silence
is a kind of voice
and can be
listened to;
and happiness,
a frank negotiation—
kibble,
his meagre price
for companionship;
companionship,
my meagre price
for love.

Had I wisdom
and the means,
I would offer
him this:
Your spirit will
live forever—
which, in dog years,
means the length
of his life,
followed by a period
of sadness
in mine,
followed by a period
of wistful
recollection,
followed by a period.

I would offer comfort,
explain that
nothing lives long
in a vacuum,
but that's okay.
Everything is
its own form
of being,

          even emptiness,
so dog endures
          as nothing less
                    than dog,
regardless of the status
          of the heart,
          the blood,
the meantime drumming.
          Change
is in the adjective alone:
good dog,
          bad dog,
                    sweet dog,
dead dog.
          You always
          will have been,
I'd tell him.

But dog has little use
          for abstract
          thought,
or even conversation.
He'll *fetch the ball,*
          and hope
that any other word
          we toss his way
                    means *food*.
          The rest is static
in the music of his day.

Had he his choice
                    of words
          he might call life
          a cage,
so bound up has it been
          in collars and
          restraints.
But for the
          thumbless inability
          to operate

a door knob,
his life is not so
different
from our own.

Except in language:
the dog can
learn
commands,
but nothing
of the frivolous,
nothing from the
ever-changing river
of abstract
colloquial
approximations,
the coinage
of our shortcuts.
How can we explain
Ooo-la-la?
How can we explain
what it means
to be in arrears?
To be over the moon
for someone?
The rules of chess?
The rules of etiquette?
The rules of war?
The dog lives
in a world
of no
explanations.

When I was ten
I used to watch
a cartoon pooch
named Mr. Peabody,
a time-traveling scientist
in horn-rimmed
glasses,

        who knew
        everything.
His sidekick was
        a boy named
        Sherman,
but he wasn't
        Sherman's dog.
I think maybe
        he was
                Plato's dog,
        the ideal template
        of the species.
Even in our present
        shadow world
                dog
        already knows
                what dog
        needs to know.
We're the ones
        with questions,
        we're the ones
unmoored
in our reality,
        always driven
                to find
                new uses
        for our
        opposable thumbs.
We lost
        our tails
                eons ago;
        now
we have only
        a finger
                to wag.

Had dog our grasp
                of syntax
        he might
explain the world

as nouns enabling verbs,
        or verbs
        propelling nouns,
while lesser
        parts of speech
        fill
                in
                the
                        gaps.

If destiny is real,
my hope is not to be
        some useless
                adverb,
pointlessly redundant
        (sic),
        in the sentence
        I
        was born
        to serve.

Yet here I am,
lolling without purpose
        in the gentle
        back-and-forth
of a groaning swing
        in my yard,
going nowhere:
                safe.
It might be
                lethargy
that keeps me here,
or entropy if you
        want to be
        cosmic about it;
but far more likely,
                fear—
        when
        free will
        reigns,

we tend to make
mistakes;
the line
is never clear
until we've crossed it.

On the other hand,
(the left one)
my opposable
but arthritic
thumb
has stopped
opposing,
a side-effect of age.
In theory,
I'm less human
for the loss.
Previously,
I've thrown
a curve ball,
opened cans,
attempted piano,
but that's
behind me now.
I can grasp
an idea,
but not a milk carton.
I can't flip a coin
while hitching a ride
out of town.
No telling
what I might do.

Or maybe that's
my truly
human side:
a willingness
to plunge
ahead
unequipped

(often with no thought
   to long-term
   consequence:
set the fire
   and fan
      the flames,
we'll clean it up
      tomorrow,
   or the day after,
   or our children will,
   or maybe we'll just
   forget about it
and find
something else
      to ruin).

But this planet
   we're riding
   into the sunset
   may be smarter
than we think.
Complacency,
   with a side order
      of hubris,
lowered our guard,
leaving us
   less vigilant,
and while we party on,
   evolution—
that implacable
bouncer—
   may be
   ushering us
   quietly
   out the door.

When I was young
   I lay in bed
   at night
   listening

to the whine of trucks
on the highway,
    reassured
        the world
would carry on
    its business
    while I slept.

These days,
I feel that same
    soft comfort
    while I wait
at the end
of a weedy lane,
        watching
    the sky turn
to black
    sparkled
        night.

Drive yourself
deep into the country
    and look up
at a dark,
    clear sky,
that vast dusting
        of stars
like sand on a beach—
but
not a beach,
        no bedrock
    of support,
no waves
    defining shore.

My mind now
    comes up short:
    I can't imagine
any kind of end to
    all that space.

(What could it
come up against?)
          I'm flummoxed
          by
infinite nothingness,
a blank
          beyond what stars
          have reached.
No distance,
no contemporary form
                    of measure
          can apply:
or maybe there is
          only distance:
the gulf between
          a place of
          no beginning
          and a place
          of no end;

either way, a birthplace;
just one beginning
          after another
as the stars intrude,
          bring movement
to a realm that
          never was before
but now
          will always be.

Oh, I don't know.

          All I can
          really say
about infinity
          comes through
          numbers:

          ten integers

of unlimited variations

which is Pi.

There's
something
circular
about it all,
and the steady measure
of the heartbeat
shapes it as
a kind of music;
the music
of the spheres,
Pythagoras called
the relative
movements
of celestial bodies.
The relative movements
of our
earthbound
bodies
carry the same
rhythms, harmonies,
discordances,
end stops.

In the grand scheme
(there's a
supposition
for you)
what I'd really like
is not to be
forsaken.

In local terms:
I'd settle
for having my old
friends back—
to wipe away

the fork
in the road
(that thoughtless lurch
toward
something unexplored,
so many lives
evaporating
like mist
behind me).

My best man Dean
(from 1982)
was one of those —
a frank contrarian
who argued
ceaselessly
about the aims of art
and whether it was
wiser in the rain
to walk or run.
A smartass and
a dumbass,
both of us believing
we were
right.
In those days,
he ironed strips
of shredded tires
to the soles
of his shoes
to keep on running.

On a cross country
drive
we met a traffic jam
outside a tunnel
on the interstate
in Pennsylvania,
and Dean
got out

to scope the scene;
he came back
with a
champaign glass,
          cut crystal,
          filled to the brim.

That was before
I was his wing man
when he first kissed
          his first wife,
                    and before
          he tried his hand
at nursing school,
          before
he got anything
published,
          and long before
          the fifteenth book,
the second-hand heart,
the big jobs
          at the big places,
the second divorce,
          and the breaking
                    of
          countless ties
                    we both
                    might have
          done well
to value more,
          as life,
with all its tar-stained
                    finality,
          steamrolled on.
          Covid
felled him in Cincinnati.
Disjuncture
          was the subject
          he liked best.

I'm thinking language is
where all
disjuncture starts:
Compass
points directions
we might go,
but
also leaves us
circumscribed
and bound.
No wonder we feel
both
hemmed-in and lost.
Place
flammable
before the mirror:
Is it now
inflammable?
Well, yes and no.

In the hurricane's
stagnant eye,
shiny grows
dull,
softness hardens,
what's hard
grows brittle
and breaks.

A puppy chases
any ball we throw,
and that's how
every love begins.
The exit,
when it comes,
levels us out
like water.

Time passes —
that's all

it knows to do.
The backyard swing
is often empty now.
The dog
is feeble,
staggers
past his bowl,
won't wag his tail,
or chase
his ball.
He stares,
baffled
by the strangeness
rising up
around him.

My words mean little
to him now,
but maybe music
stands a chance:
that poetry
of calculated sound,
a phenomenon
that navigates
straight
to the right side
of the brain,
no filters of
left brain language
to buffer
the experience
with shades of
our uncertainty;
harmonious
or discordant,
major or minor;
infinite variations
from a limited scale,
various as Pi,
though sometimes

inadvertently redundant—
George Harrison's
"My Sweet Lord"
identical to
"He's So Fine"
by the Chiffons.
But musical or
literary,
both are compositions;
emotions, too,
when we
compose ourselves:
all three an attempt
to bring
order
out of nothingness.

Meanwhile,
the new coffee maker
makes sounds
I don't understand,
something
like a leaf-blower
in a distant
block,
and produces coffee
that doesn't suit
my taste.
But I drink it
because
the machine
is mine
and paid for.
In several ways
that sums up
who I am.
How about you?

The thumb
is one kind

of machine,
and so is
every other
part of us,
and machines
are capable of
every possibility
but one:
the stay is finite.

This day is finite.

And that's
the cradle
of philosophy.

Science tells us
what will happen
in a billion years,
but still next week
is anybody's
guess,
so let's not
tell the mirror
how impressed
we are.

Night-sweats again
last night,
which might mean
anything,
or nothing,
since the body
likes to
leave us guessing.
Have I been
snacking
on toxins?
Pain pills might be
the culprit,

since relief will often
punish us
with side-effects.

The brain remembers
comfort
better than it
conjures up
old ills,
so last week's hammer
to the thumb
can't hurt you now.
Abstractions, too,
evaporate
unless you take the time
to make them real,
so
dibs
on that brilliant
thought
you had the other day
and then forgot.

And all the others
you'll neglect,
since that's the trap
you've trained
your mind
to set.
Laziness, in the end,
will cost you everything.
Me, too,
of course.

In his last play
Shakespeare said
we're all just
dream particles,
and so did The Crew Cuts
in their 1954 hit

"Sh-Boom,"
and so did
E. O. Lyte
in his 1881
chart-topper
"Row, Row, Row
Your Boat."

Exhibit A is time,
so dogged in its work.
But
if we're just a dream,
in trains of thought
are we
the passengers
or engineers?

In Schrödinger's Universe
we're both
until we find out
the true state
of the box.

Mathematics is
a door
that opens inward:
imagine Pi to be
the universal genome,
granting us
uniqueness
on an infinite and
non-repeating string.

Furthermore (uh-oh,
lecturing again),
without the tilt
of our imperfect globe
there'd be
no spring
to counterweight

        the fall.
                Life's
        blueprint
is a side-effect
                of
wobble.

Before the tines
        of agriculture
dug the plot,
        we had
        no word
                for weed.
Then science
parceled plants
        in proper rows.
And yes,
        the ground
        turned chemical,
                but oh
the green looks nice,
and big tomatoes,
        freed from
        limitations
                of taste,
gleam perfect red
        in fluorescent
        grocery-store sun.

I took a fall
        yesterday—
walked out
        the back door
toting a box
that blocked my view,
        stepped where
the porch planks
had been removed
        to fix the rot.
Found out I still

have great
reflexes.
Also,
great reflexes
aren't enough.

But that's the
up and down
of day by day:
a buddies trip
to someplace
new,
a broken copier,
a strip-mall
colonoscopy,
a daughter from Seattle
flying in,
her infant son
aglow
with each
discovery.
It's life's uneven
edge
that keeps it
close to glorious.

The shivering trees
rain leaves
amid
November rain.
But the dead limb
can't drop
what's left,
and after all those
yearly rings
of grief,
can only reach out
ghostly
to a steely sky.

Change is
never-changing
in its cutthroat ways,
and so
to every almost-love
whose path
I failed to follow
in some lost
cacophonous spring,
I offer
one sad truth:
illusion is the mainstay
of all youth,
as hard
as that my be
for us to swallow.

Even past seventy,
I find
new disturbances
rolling in from
the everyday world:
not
the rain-slicked road
itself,
with that carpet of
acorns
downed by storm,
but the indecision
I read
in the last hesitation
of the squirrel
I barely felt
beneath
the front left tire.

Some words exist as
verb or noun.
Regret is one.
And love,

            of course.
And longing.
No dictionary
            here required.
We know regret
            is just a wall
encircling our mistakes;
that love
            is just
                        a search
            for gateways
            in the wall;
that
            longing
is many things,
but mostly
the ladder we
            ascend
            to see
beyond our reach.

Infallibility, on the other
            human hand,
belongs more
            to nature than
                        to popes,
            more to physics
            than
            philosophy.
Sometimes
            my computer
tells me I am
            not connected
            to the outside
                        world:
it's never wrong.

But the nature
                        of physics
            is cold,

and the physics
of nature
beats with no heart
to drive it.
We yearn for
balance,
but remain
baffled between
shortcomings
and talents,
no bridge
to cross
the chasm,
no explanations
for who
or why
we are.

We all have things
we love
to hate
and things
we hate
to love,
but the universe
is not
our therapist.
We claim to like
those flowers
bursting into bloom

along the creek bed,
while pollen
keeps us sniveling,
pouring out
buckets
of meaningless tears.

This morning Ari said
In my next life

I want to be
an empty shadow
on a bridge.
He's not yet nine.

My next life
holds less clarity,
although my past
still pushes
stark reminders:
ten years back,
I broke thick ice
in water troughs
and with bare hands
fished out the
jagged chunks
to let the horses drink.
The pain of it
still halts me,
the killing stiffness
that settled in
before the fingers
all
went numb.

Or maybe
that's genetics.
Arriving,
we already
own a parcel
of surprises.
From my mother:
a taste for licorice.
From my father:
a tendency
toward
light-footed laughter.
My grandparents
gifted me
an understanding

that the mirror
is no one's friend.
Show it your face,
and it returns
no truth
but the reverse of it.

Longing
has brought civilization
to its peak,
but binds us up
in sleepless nights;
undermines
our faith
in what we build,
but drives us,
after disappointments
numerous
and dire,
to keep on
building
toward the far side
of the sun.
How silly we are.

The mind expands
from *what* to *why*
dividing us,
in theory,
from the beasts,
who care more
about the next meal
than arguing
philosophy,
In nature,
it's enough
to know
the sun
comes up—
no need

to do the math.
The dog
does not act
startled
when the porch lights
flicker on
or when
we put him in the car
and speed
the highway.
Sure,
the vacuum cleaner
makes him bark
or slink away,
but that's his only
unsolved mystery.

The human state
is one of
escalating needs.
We rise
from bland simplicities—
a piece of fruit,
a cave,
a scraped
wrap of fur—
into towers of longing:
air-conditioned
walk-in closets
overflowing with
our ancestors'
lace tablecloths,
plus
high-speed internet
to keep us
in the know.
And a tailored
wrap of fur.

Symphonic music
        fills
        the opera house,
criminals
        the jailhouse,
while row after row
        of row houses
        house
our lesser selves.

Today I ate tacos
        in an otherwise
        empty restaurant,
and a man
        in baggy jeans
entered by a side door,
        stuffed his pickets
with ketchup packets
                and fled.
        On the drive home
I saw,
for the third time,
        a red fox
        standing by
        the roadside,
drawn
        by the
lingering scent
        of its kit,
struck there
early in the week
and hauled away
        by agents
                of the county.
The sadness
        of the fox
is not the same
        as my sadness
        for the fox,
or my sadness for

        the ketchup thief,
        but all of us
I'm sure,
are bound up
        somehow
        in the same
sad mystery,
with longing
        at its core.

Aunt Doris searched
        for love
but wound up
        hoarding
                glass
        collectibles.
Uncle Harold
        thought his
        salesman job
depended on
        his jokes.
He opened up new
        territories,
but so much
        forced laughter
        left him
friendless
        in the company,
and after forty years
        they told him
        to go home.

But better not to dwell
        on others'
        quiet tragedies.
And so the
        crossword puzzle
dominates
        our thoughts
        through lunch,

                        taunting us
with hints
of words
            we might not
                        even know.
            But that's okay.
It's nice
            to take a
            holiday
            from narrative.
It's nice
            to overlook
            how all
            the stories end.

One female firefly
            flashes
            a false signal
to attract a
different species
            she will have
            for lunch,
but I still love
the flashes at dusk,
            mostly yellow,
            sometimes green.
I've heard one species
            flashes red,
which seems alarming,
and Asheville
            for two weeks
            in the year
plays host to the rare
            blue ghost,
but I'm not making
any pilgrimage.
            There's plenty
            to see
without searching.
Never doubt it.

Doubt is the dandelion
in the meadow,
a soft
but sturdy flower,
more yellow
than the sun.
Admire it
all day long,
but pull its head
by nightfall,
or tomorrow you will
meet its
spectral self,
a globe of airy spikes
dismantling
in the breeze,
spreading its
broadleaf trouble
everywhere,
strangling whatever's
weak and green.

Sometimes when I
watch the news,
I think of
dandelions
in our DNA:
shaping us as
drifting spirits
of destruction,
desperate on the hunt
to fill our time.
The malls close down,
the young
refuse to grow.
Tall buildings waste
a multitude
of floors.
No wonder

we declare
so many wars.

Sometimes I have to
say a thing
to know
if I believe it.
Testing that
hypothesis:
Old pains
are more tolerable
than new.
My first thought:
true.
But what about
the one
that nags its way
into your heart,
deeper and deeper,
year after year?
For me not much
is clear
past basic math.
We want to know
which fork in the trail
is right,
but maybe that
depends on
what comes next,
the way a note of
music
can't be right or wrong
until you
hear the notes
that follow.

Dawn is in the next room
encouraging
a friend
who wants to

go into
the hat-band
business.
She's a muse
by nature,
a mental
lifeguard
keeping
many heads
above the waterline.
Meanwhile,
I'm here
stewing over
past failures,
all the loves
that launched
so easily then sank.
Her presence is
the comfort
that sustains me,
even when her mind
is somewhere else.
All love
is a blind leap,
and the landing
can be
soft or hard;
lucky or lethal.
I've danced and suffered
all extremes,
and see
it has to be that way:
Who can
really know
what drive's
another's heart?
I lucked out
in the end,
and found there's
bliss in

dogged domesticity.
And furthermore:

If there's a dog
in your life,
    you're lucky.
If there are two dogs
    in your life,
    the dogs
        are lucky.

But how much
of anything
        is luck?

Down to my last dollar,
    stranded,
two thousand miles
from home,
    I walked into
a place along
    the Vegas strip
and called the color
    right
    for nine
    straight
    turns
        of a wheel.
The House
    believed
    in lucky streaks
    and put
a different croupier
    in place
to staunch the flow.
    I read the
        signs
and rode my
    winnings home.
    So call it

luck,
I guess.
It felt like
something
bigger
at the time.

Or luck is an illusion:
each
flip of a coin
revealing turns
of destiny,
and seers really see,
and the Tarot,
the I Ching
give glimpses
of what
is
and therefore
has to be.

Last year I paused
before a dash
across the road,
but stopped myself.
A speeding car
erupted
from a blind spot;
by luck or intuition,
hesitation
kept my blood
contained in
its machine.

In Scottish Lowlands
once
I trespassed
on a farmer's land
to see some
standing stones,

and stepped
into a peat bog
at the low end
of the field,
my toddling daughter
in my arms.
I tossed her back
to those behind,
and went on
sinking
by myself.
The power of the pull
made clear
I may have made
a final step.

But two feet down
I stopped,
and in the end lost
nothing
but my shoes.
That muck
diverted us.
We veered away
from Locherbie
minutes before
the bomb
rained wreckage
from the sky.
Eleven in the village
died,
my loved ones
not among them.

Good luck?
Not everyone's.
Is that the
necessary
balance then?

Horatio was chided
        by his friend
        for thinking small —
more things
in heaven
and earth,
                et cetera —
        But Hamlet
        was a
        condescending
        college kid,
given to
rash pronouncements
        and a willingness
to believe in ghosts.
He dithered
        till it got him
        dead.
The smart one
was Horatio,
        who knew a hawk
        from a handsaw,
no matter
the direction
of the wind.

Both:
endowed by
        their creator
        with certain
        inalienable rights
to a personality.
Consider the word's
vacuity,
it's plea for adjectives
to give it substance:
        shy
        outgoing
        vivacious
        obnoxious

charming —
but personhood
is not required.
Our dogs
cats,
horses,
all have personalities,
we say —
one reason
we don't eat them.
If given half a chance
that cow
that pig
might show some
human traits,
but they've been cast
as
beef and bacon,
staples
that predate
the Piggly Wiggly.
Chickens, too —
dumb clucks —
and the unblinking fish
because they
clearly
are
not
us.
Be thankful for whatever
personality
you have;
it saves you
from the slaughterhouse

People do
eat venison,
but all the kids
love Bambi,
so deer get

        dispensations:
we reap them
        one by one,
no processing plants
allowed.
So too with
        pheasant,
        duck,
        elk,
        bear
        and dove.
Game animals,
        we call them,
(without irony)
and make up rules
to keep them safe.
        Except when
they're in season.

A thousand
generations
        back,
        kill or be killed
was the law;
        today it's
        kill or be
embarrassed
by the lack of
        taxidermied heads
        above the
        door frames.

We're all hunters,
        though
        not everyone
        hunts.
To fill the void
        we knit scarves,
join bowling leagues,
do volunteer work.

Some drink
until their smiles
curl
unembittered
toward the dark.

A slatted swing
can be a comfort
only briefly.
Flies accumulate,
and so we rise again,
joints aching
against inertia,
heart gulping blood.

Forget repose —
those calm
blue days
will get us in the end.
A touch of chaos
keeps the landscape
green.

That gray unruly sky
is one more form
of thinking;
each bright bolt
a thought
inflicting change.

So revel in whatever
seems unsettled.
Storms are here
to keep us
building shelters;
shelters grant us
time to reach
toward reachable
dreams.
The unreachables,

of course,
require
much stronger
dreaming.

We're trapped here,
naturally:
this fragile sphere
our exile
and our home.
But that
might not
be the end of it.

The mind has insights
it can't
understand.
A stroke can
leave the brain
dyslexic,
as I've said,
jumbling
strings of letters,
sometimes
skipping
words
entirely,
cancelling intentions,
overleaping meanings.

If only
we could proofread
our behavior,
revise our blunders
before the world
gets wind
of what we've done.

That's one idea of
heaven,

I suppose —
infinite do-overs,
allowing all the turns
that we may need.

Or maybe that's what
purgatory is.

But Latin says
one turn
per universe
is all we get,
so let's not wreck
this train
on the fine points
of religion,
which,
in the wrong hands,
is a battering ram.
Even passive forms
turn brutal
when control
is up for grabs.
I admire
the Buddhist's
eightfold path
of compassionate care
for all,
even bugs,
but that's just
in the brochures.
In Sri Lanka,
Buddhists
waged war
against the Tamil
and fifty thousand died.

If the founders
of religions had
thought things through

they might have
kept their
mouths shut.
No matter
how beautiful
a path might be,
human nature will
always
intervene
to say
it can be
made better
with a bulldozer.

I still believe in dog
in all its forms.

If prodigies
are born to
revolutionize,
What happens to
musicians
born too soon?
Say your DNA
blessed you
to be
the uncontested genius
of the slide trombone,
but
it was only
the fifth century?
Would you sense
what was missing?
Would the absence
of your instrument
drive you mad?

Are those we count
unhinged or
out of step

just born too early
or too late
to know their gifts?
The time is out of joint,
said Hamlet.
Maybe in another era
he could have
invented shag carpeting
or the electric doorbell.
He might have been
your local
weatherman.
Or at least a
fictional version thereof.

But here's a question:
now that time
is back in joint,
is Shakespeare
any more real to us
than Hamlet,
Romeo,
Lady MacBeth?
The author
or the work:
which is the
enduring dream?

Okay, Nature,
Shakespeare
says,
Inspire me.
Not my job,
says Nature.
Find your
own way
out of town.

I worry
that I've had

no thought
a billion others
haven't thought before,
or done a thing
that once was good
but isn't anymore.

Given a choice between
breadth
of knowledge
or
depth
of understanding,
choose neither,
which is the same
as depth
of understanding,
which always
contradicts
the parts you
think you know.

Then remember a time
when you were six,
a red bicycle
in late December,
the one waited for,
longed for,
and there it
suddenly was,
and in a cold rain
you wheeled it
down the sidewalk
and rode it,
wobbling,
not minding the chill,
the wet,
happier
than you'd ever been
in a way

less complicated
than you might ever
know again.

Later that day
your mother would
borrow a neighbor's bike
to ride along
behind you
in the empty,
gravel-strewn street,
and your wheels
would slip
and dump you
on the skinning pavement,
and your mother,
ignorant of hand brakes,
would
peddle
backward
as she ran
over your head.
Then
the jerky car ride,
the dim
emergency room
where a stranger
would sew a part of
your face
together again,

but even so, it's still
the joy
of the morning
that endures,
dominates,
despite the temporary
setback of the
afternoon.

The mind levels,
according to need.

Some days you will
stand in line
longer
than those behind you.
Ignore the
inexplicability.
Plant tomatoes
on a frosted
morn;
trust
the vines
will
find their way.

No matter how much
see
or
think
or
know
we pocket against
bad turns,
we will always wonder
what's missing.
In that sense,
we will stand in line
forever.

Consider this:
when two circles
touch,
the point of contact
would be infinitesimal,
beyond molecular,
in fact,
as both sides of

both halves
curve infinitely away.

So why
no great explosion,
no splitting
of the atom
whenever one thing
bumps
another?

Even in
casual contact,
electrons ought to
register collision,
circling,
as they do,
at 4.8467 million
miles per hour.

I didn't make
that number up,
by the way;
some math
or physics person
did,
and its
precision
makes it
something
we believe.

So
if subatomic particles
meet with
devastating speed,
their combined
momentum
ought to cause
a catastrophic

rupture
in the fabric,
a chain reaction
blowing us
to smithereens.

And yet it doesn't.

Some
barrier
we struggle
to define
restrains the
cataclysmic rift,
creates a buffer,
the way a magnet
invisibly repels
its polar twin.

How do we
account for that?
What force
maintains
the calm
against calamity?

What keeps the chaos
momentarily
at bay?
What ingredient
saves us
every second
of the day?

That mystery
is the real
mystery.

So what if
flies accumulate

around our
leavings?
At least we're here
to wonder.

For now, anyway.
I've reached an age
at which
a magazine subscription
is a sign
of optimism,
and the past
is not
a country road
meandering
but an
expressway
jammed with wrecks.

Time is the table
where I place
my meager bets,
and
life staggers uphill
through a landscape
level as the sea.
Logic is sometimes
useless,
is what I mean.
Remember Icarus:
his story grew from
simple logic —
the closer we get
to the sun,
the hotter
it must be.
But that's
flatlander thinking,
and any
mountaineer

could have set
the storyteller straight:
          that the higher
          you climb,
the colder your fate
                    will be.

In Alaska
          a convocation
          of eagles
squabbles over salmon
                    by a stream.
          Thirty below,
they snatch
          each other's shreds
          of fish,
sometimes slipping
from the bank
          into the
          ravening flow.
But instantly they rise,
                    a flurry of
          beaks and claws,
          the ice balls
clumped along
their wings
          failing to
          weigh them down.

We all know
borderline survival,
                    the struggle
          to stay aloft
amid assassins
          hungry as ourselves.

One frozen afternoon
          I plowed my
oversized
          leaf blower

through three acres
 of deep sheddings,
clearing out a season's
 wet debris
 from forty oaks.

The effort stoked
 a feeding frenzy
 in my blood,
so much
 it might have
laid me out
for good.
 No rapids rage
 across my yard,
but a gully
 slashes
through the wooly slope
 and when it rains
 the narrow bed
 clogs fast
with everything
 a storm can bring.

 These leaves
are one more sign
 of my undoing,
and I can let them
 rot in place,
 or I can feed them
to a whirlwind
of my own making,
 hoping
they will clear the fence
 along the highway
and never
 blow back.

Today,
out walking a

gravelled curve,
I saw a grand gazebo,
screened, ornate —
an overdone
birdcage in a
scrappy stand of scrub.
Up close,
it bore
the tatter
of neglect,
a dead starling
hollowed
on the floor.

Chaos
is our word
for disparities
beyond
our understanding.
Nothing real
is random.
Everything contributes.

Here's the arrival of death
expressed as a
linguistic dislocation:

nowhere
is
now here

Books I'll never read
collect
around me;
knowing they're
within my reach
provides a promise,
and sometimes
promises

can be enough.
The clearest lessons
are more concrete.
If the mind says
you can do a thing
but the body says
you can't,
listen to the body.

If a fifth-year oak
grows
from the rock foundation
of your house,
do not
bring out the axe.
Foundations need
protecting,
but when the sun
scorches grass
and stones
burn hot,
each swing
of a dull blade
will disappoint.
The pounding
in your ears
will hammer
the brain,
and drop you
on your back
like a heavyweight.
Concerns will shift
from
household care,
to bad decisions made,
and where
to send
the flowers.

A lot can happen
    in a single turn.
Everything, in fact.

Still and all,
a few particulars
stand out:
    I won things
        at the fair,
    so there's that.
I watched a full circle
    double-rainbow
    fill a rain-gray sky
    in North Carolina
    and felt stared at
by something like God—
    not judgmentally,
    but as an object
    of mild curiosity.

I've been delighted
    by coincidence
    enough to know
it always lurks
        nearby.

I've had dogs
    who needed me
        and cats
    who
    found me useful.

I saw the zoo
    when I was still
        too young
to see the sadness,
and the carnival,
    with its miracle
    of lights
and whirling cages

and overlapping
music
spilling
through the night.

I've trudged up
flights of stairs
with small daughters
sitting
on my boots.

I've felt warm sun
on a cold day,
and a cool breeze
on a hot one.

Water when thirsty,
food when hungry,
a place
to lie down when
day has
wrung me out.

And friends.
And loves.

So never mind
the rest of it.

The white oak
sheds
acorns
in a
six-year cycle;
the red oak,
more reckless
to flower,
showers
acorns
every second year.

More acorns
means
more saplings
plundering
the ground,
starving out
the roots
of older growth.

Both squirrel and deer
prefer the leavings
of the white —
a sweeter,
less acidic nut —
and thin the crop
before
it settles in to root.

The upshot of
the white oak's
great withholding
and the sharing
of the fruit:
an extra
hundred years
beyond the red.

Measure your seasons,
says nature,
and for every turn
you take
give a little back.

On the other hand,
there are times
to wallow,
so be sure
to do it right —
let the weight
of the word

transport you
back and forth
between
the muddy banks
of the slough.
Let the sound of it
guide you to
its meaning:
movement
freed
from destination,
a squirm
without anguish,
a rocking,
rolling word,
a play-pit
fit
for the child inside.
Don't think of it
as piggish, or
a word with
aftermath attached:
(self-pity,
misery,
grief)
Don't think in terms
of dark
surrender,
but let it rise from
its own depths
through some happy
recollection:
the day you
walked the shallows
of the shore
looking
for sand dollars or
beach glass,
delighting
in the soft pull

of the sea
beneath
your feet,
the crystalized earth
giving way,
bit by bit,
to accommodate
your being there,
even as the
new wave
came washing in.

Or racing downhill
through the woods,
launching yourself
from fallen
logs,
leaping the
undergrowth,
trusting
there would always
be a place to land,
before the next
high-arcing vault,
and the next,
and the next,
your speed electric
with momentum,
so much faith
you might as well
be flying.

Yes, that's the feeling.
Now turn the word
back
upon itself
the way a
mirror would:
wallow in it.

I feel a meditation
coming on,
or else
the mirror of one:

Even with a trillion billion
stars shining,
space remains
dark.
Empty is invisible;
light lights
what's there,
and nothing else;
and everything
we see
is just
reflection
carried
by the light.
Conclusion:
light
is the mirror
the universe uses
to see itself.

As you see
I'm fishing for
something deeper
than a tuna sandwich.
Mortality, etc.
This week I took a trip
to my hometown.
At the the mortuary
I ordered
my gravestone
(I like to
stay ahead
of things).
Kept to the family form:
name and date only

(one yet to be
determined).
But in Sunday's game
of
choose your
epitaph,
I'd opt for this:
How rude
of me —
you've come
all this way
to visit
and here I am
not
paying
attention.

At the big hotel
on the highway
south
of town
(four stories,
tallest building
in the county)
they had a pool
in the courtyard
with the depth
stenciled
in black paint
on the concrete edge:
4 feet, 12 inches;
then further along,
5 feet, 15 inches.
I don't doubt
the accuracy.
They're the people
I come from.

A dog's life ago
I had a roadblock

in my blood.
          It's been a
          long haul back,
                    and, sure,
I lost some luggage
on the way,
          but most of me
          survives,
and writing this
is one way
          I can calculate
          how much.

We've all got
the same argument
          with time.
Each year
it gets tougher
          to gather
                    thoughts
          and put on socks.
          Maybe by the end

I'll be limited to
          long
                    unbroken
          strings
          of
          pregnant
          pauses.

We're an ornery species,
          and mayhaps
(a fine word,
long unused)
                    the threat
                    of heaven
is what sends us
          straight to hell.

Sure, rainbows
bolster smiles,
even
without
the pot of gold,
but black light
shines
beyond the visible.
The spectrum
broadens
out of sight —
another minor sadness.
Magic isn't magic
if we see
the way it works.

Some mornings,
it's the
blue jay's call
reeling
through the chill;

some mornings,
it's a child's
abandoned ball
half-hidden
in the weeds;

some mornings,
it's root canal.

Today's mystery:
a dead
hummingbird
on the kitchen floor,
it's
iridescent green
gone drab
against the linoleum.
I'd like

an explanation,
            though
            results
speak for themselves:
some untoward form
            of truth
has triumphed
            over beauty.
                        Yet again.
Our daily search
for things
worth keeping
            blunders on.
The world is always
                        falling
            away from us,
so we hold on
to what we can:
            we're hoarders,

            and
since flowers
                        never last
            we pile up
            things that do.

But what's a diamond
to a dog?

            No child
            would swap
                        a puppy
                        for a rock.
That's comes later,
            when growth
brings complications,
and cows become
            more viable
than magic beans.
We go for X-rays

and
the technician
puts lead shields
around our heart.

The heart
is made for giving,
but that's not
what a hoarder
does.
We hold
our losses close
and stack up bricks
to keep them safe.
The child
succumbs to ledgers
and appointments,
No playing
in the yard
with dog,
just training it to
act like
something else.

Some say they see
the future
in a busy sky,
some claim
a person's palm
holds everything.
That's how I learned
to shrug.
Why fear
what's out there?
Imagination
makes room
for monsters,
milkweed,
and brass chandeliers.
One way or another

everything
comes true.
Symbol is
as symbol does.
If you hunger
for a
fairy tale,
try that one.
The core of
human comedy
is hope,
the product
of its tragedy.

And speaking of
the Arts,
forget Aristotle,
that smug
bean-counter
who pioneered
the job of
filing clerk.

But dibs on Plato,
so misunderstood;
he had no beef
with poets,
just saw
that in Utopia
there'd be no need.
What cemetery
keeps an ambulance
on call?

We teach our kids
who won the wars,
but outcomes
barely sketch
the monster's shadow.
Winning is no

badge of validation.
Tomorrow's fires
may yet
burn down the town.

My great-grandfather,
J. Bunyan Smith,
designer of the
Coca Cola bottle,
was named for a
famous writer
but I never saw him
touch a book.
For him, the only
good line
ended with a
bated hook.
He taught me
how to run
the steely curve
half the length
of the worm's
body
so the fish
could be surprised.
The child I was
cried
when it snagged
my finger,
the barb
digging in deep
and holding.

Crying is
a native tongue
of children,
and I spoke it often:
when I plunged
over handle bars;
when a rock

split my lip;
when my
first few dogs
were killed
(car, mail truck,
garbage truck, poison).

But pain
no longer
brings on tears.
Instead,
I cry at gestures
of goodwill,
of unforced stooping
to another's need,
or any sign
we still possess
the empathetic gene.

But nature
is still out there.
I think of stories
in the news
of small dogs
wandering too close
to the swamp.
For longer
than we know,
the alligator
has held steady
to its ways:
clamp down,
drag under,
wait.

We share the impulse
not to leave the
warm waters of
our feeding ground,
but now and then

we go upright,
openhanded,
opposable thumb
and all,
and separate
ourselves
from the
cold blooded.
We're capable
of
offering.

But surveys tell us
three of four
Americans
mistrust
three of four
Americans.
You do the math.

We can at least agree
the world is full
of overlooks,
grand vistas
of blue mountains
across the way,
or blue lakes
on the valley floor,
or blue skies
tufted with cirrus
as the sun
goes down.

Views from the summit
are okay
if beauty
is your bailiwick,
but postcards
won't convey

the sense
          of having climbed.

Language is
a view
          from
a kind of summit;
          also
          a kind of climb;
or it's the mountain
                    itself,
          or the lake,
          or the sky—
whatever
          simile or
          metaphor
                    you choose.
Language,
          like the universe,
          contains all things,
which is a paradox.
The first contains
          the second
          which contains
                    the first.
Do abstractions
          come to us
          through language,
or
          are wishes
          a product
of the Big Bang?
          What about hope?
What about irrationality?
          What about
          misspellings?
          Is
                    language
                    describing
                    language

setting
mirror
against
mirror,
reflecting
nothing
but the nothing
of itself?
I guess words
are never
the whole story.
A visit to the jungle
is more
than just
the slide show
afterwards.

Now, the verbal:
The soft voice
is typically
the wisest,
but
we listen to
the loud,
so if you can't
be smart,
crank up
the volume:
that's how tyrants
get things done.

Writers tend to be
a quiet bunch,
either because
they weigh
their words
with care
or they're afraid
of being bullied

like they were
in junior high.

In Plato's Cave
would language
be the object
or the shadow,
or the fire
behind them both?
Or maybe language
is the exit
from the cave.

Plato put no
mirrors
on those walls,
but writers
can't resist
reflection
and its pretense
to the ownership
of light.
That's why
in poems
the moon
comes up more often
than the sun.

That cold
inconstant face
is
inspiration,
waxing
and
waning
like the rest of us.
Horace, Dryden,
Tacitus, Cicero:
the list goes on

of those
whose words meant
something
once
but fail today to muster
double-digit
bookstore sales.
In that regard
I'm doing well.
My work
is just as
dusty and obscure
as any long-dead
what's-his-name.
Probably more so.

But language
shows better in
application
than in theory,
and the words I need
this afternoon
are those
to tell me
how many wraps of
plumber's tape
will seal a
shower head
connection.

The biggest mirror
is usually
in the bathroom.

The conundrum
of the mirror:
the thing it
never
shows us

is the surface of itself,
revealing only
what the light allows.
What is it
when the room
is dark?
Not a mirror
anymore, but
something nameless;
not the reverse
of darkness,
but part of it.

I cut my hair today,
standing before
the bathroom mirror,
which states my
independence
from society's routines.
But still I worry
people will
look at me
funny.
Even with a pair of
mirrors
so I could see the
back of my head,
I never
made it look
quite
right.

When I was five,
the barber cut my hair
for a quarter.
I remember the sound
of his clippers,
its soothing
vibration against
skull.

I remember the feel
of the cloth
he draped
over me, and
the padded,
elevated steel chair
that propped me up.
I remember the smell
of Vitalis,
and of something
like vanilla cookies.
I remember the coatrack
by the door,
the jar of combs,
the row of
dark wooden chairs.
I remember the giant
mirror
on the wall
and all that it reflected.

Why would the mind
hold on
to that,
but not
to what I had for lunch
last Tuesday?

Each generation
first wants
the world
to change
then be the way it was.

Also at five I got
a Daisy BB gun,
like my cousins,
and got shot
multiple times,

though
never lost an eye.
At twelve
they gave us
.410 shotguns
capable of killing
anything.
Our mothers
tossed us car keys and
sent us to the store
for smokes.
No childproofing then,
of cabinets
or bottles;
no seatbelts,
no lifeguards
at the creek,
no worries about playing
whiffle ball
under streetlights
late into the night;

a world of
old refrigerators
dumped in the woods —
death traps
for suffocation.
Construction sites
strewn with
stray blasting caps
in every block;
above us
linemen
stringing miles
of multicolored wires
through treetops
so every house
could have a phone.

The town square
        still had
        hitching posts.

Our cautionary myths
        were rabid dogs
                or else
        the Naked Man
        who waited
                in the dark
                woods,
        or maybe
                in the bushes
        by the porch.

We lived for summer
                truck rides
        to the hardware store,
        the feed warehouse,
        the farm at the
south end of the county,
                that soothing
                traveling wind
        the only time
        the summer heat
        would let us breathe.

The oldest got
        the running boards,
        one boy per side,
arms hooked
                through the
        red Ford's
        shot-out windows,
                while the girls
        and younger boys
stood swaying
        in the pickup's
        straw-strewn bed,

basking
in the streaming breeze
above the roofline.

Punishments:
a willow switch
across bare legs,
or leather belt
through denim,
or sometimes
two-days' work
in August heat
unloading feed corn
from a darkened,
snake-infested crib.

The best ride
took the
two-lane highway
out of town,
a swerving trip
across the state line
to buy fireworks
at a roadside stand:
woven strings
of Black Cats,
and sparklers
showering
cold fire,
but also
cherry bombs
and M-80s,
enough black powder
to remove a hand.
I know the feel of
holding the
stubby silver tube,
the lit fuse blazing down,
discovering
in myself

how long I dared
before the throw.

In memory:
not a closed fist
in my brain,
but
broad smiles
and laughter.
We all were
giants then,
cock-sure
and careless,
goading each new day
to try and stop us
if it could,
to knock us
from our hard-won
stance
atop the hill.

Not everyone
would make it
to fifteen.

Times change.
We keep our young
in bubblewrap
and line their walls
with
warning lights
and caution tape.

The pendulum blade
cuts
at both extremes,
so protection
is what leaves us
unprotected
in the end.

Choppy waters
make for
better sailors.
A good life
calls for more
disruption
than the mirrored surface
of a stagnant pond.

I've had friends
who thought
deeply,
thoroughly,
and are dead now.
But
key thoughts
survive,
spur my own mind to
keep
trudging.
Even now
they keep me
plighted
to a game that
ultimately ends
where it began:
a cry
in the light.

Our parents screwed
us up,
we think,
denying how much
fault is ours.
Don't offer up
old wounds
on a silver tray.
We can't grow up
without forgiving

everything that lies
                    behind us.

I took a drive up north
          to my father's grave
          and found
the plot adjoining his
          was newly occupied—
          sold
          by my stepmother
to forever hold
a woman
my father never met.
          No gravesite
          to the left or right,
just the two of them
          laid out like
          a pair of
          lifelong lovers,
their tombstones
          not five inches
          apart.
I did some research,
          found we
were in high school
          together.

Somehow it helped
          to know
          our histories
ran parallel.
I don't know why
          I found
          this stranger's
          presence
          so unsettling.
We're all figments
of the same
          community.

So what do we
owe the past,
anyway?
Nothing but our
thanks.

I can't remember
my first question,
whether
before or after
being pushed out
into the first world
of a bright hospital room,
but either way
it was probably
the same question
I have now:

What is all this?

I had
no words,
no syntax then
to guide my gut,
so maybe that question
was just a piece
of punctuation:
!?
meaning,
of course,
Wonder,
and wonder
is a question
that never
stops asking.

Then language sets in,
with its
faltering power
to command:

No!
says the mother, and
baby must stop;
No!
says the baby
but no one stops.
No-no-no-no-no
chants the baby,
but still no one stops.
The fists tighten,
the feet kick,
the baby squirms
in utter rejection
of the world,
the primal language
erupts,
loud and chaotic,
a full and tearful
tantrum,
but still no one listens,
and baby
wonders:

Why does language
not always work?

The question endures.

Free as the wind,
they say,
but the wind
is always bound
by its own channel
of flow.

Today I saw a tight
chattering
of starlings,
a hundred or so,
whipping

through the sky,
        angling in concert,
                haphazardly,
                but together,
tossing
        like a tissue
        on a windy day,
        though the day
                was calm.

When I was young,
        I saw a
        congregation
migrating north,
                tens of tens
                of thousands,
filling a narrow corridor
        of summer air,
fifteen minutes
in the passing.
        A glorious sight,
        except to farmers
at the end of day,
                praying
        that their fields
might not
        become a spot
        of respite
                for a frenzy
of ravenous birds.

Two takes
        on the same
        full sky,
two forms
        of impact
        on the heart.

But why do this,
        or anything?

To undercut
the feeling
of a wasted life.
To turn reflection
into
portraiture.

Language and mirror:
language is
a mirror
we look through;
mirrors
are a language
that looks back.

All trains have
sidetracks,
branch lines,
they're called,
and here
such detours
from the main
reflect the past.

My first encounters
taught me nature
was no friend:
the prickly pears
that dotted
the back yard,
the swarm
of hornets
I discovered
in a neighbor's
stack of
cinder blocks.
I had no words,
but pain
evoked a lexicon
more ancient,

shrill and inarticulate.
    But no one
    answered,
so I stopped.

The prickly pears
    were easy:
I could
pluck the needles out
myself.
    But hornets
    brought havoc
a two-year-old
    could not
    address alone:
I found my father
    sleeping
    on the couch;
        he packed
        wet tobacco
    on the stings
    to stem the hurt.
To my surprise,
    it drew the fire
        away.

Language has its limits:
People and dogs
        dissemble.
    The dog knows
    the food
    on the counter
        is not
    to be taken,
but takes it anyway,
    hangs his head
in shame when caught.
    People:
    same deal.
Both species:

owned
by their society.

Cats
have no rules,
act
only for themselves.
The dog will save
the drowning child,
the cat
will watch
with half-interest
while licking its paw
on the grassy bank.
Love the dog, because
it needs you to;
respect the cat
because it doesn't.

Each evening we
go out to
walk the dog,
who sniffs each inch
of ground
as if she's
on the trail
of a dog's
wealth
of mystery.
And yet she sniffed
her way past the
hare
poised on
its haunches
not four feet
to her right.
Another sixty yards
of keeping
her nose
to the path

and she missed
the fawn
    stumbling by
    on a trail
        parallel
    to our own,
barely a
    loud whisper away.
What
    search propelled
    her,
so focussed
    and persevering,
but still so ignorant of
    discoveries
    easily made?
Maybe she had
    bigger
    scents
    to track:
I've seen old
    copperheads
    along this route.
The rain last night
    might have
set them
scavenging.

Apparent *non sequitur*
    (though it isn't*):*
Where does art
come from?
    the polite woman

at the cocktail party
        asks.
It comes from
shopping at
    the L.L. Bean Store
    in Freeport, Maine

            at 3 a.m.,
or tripping on
the sidewalk,
            or finding
            a dead robin
in a swimming pool,
            or forgetting
            where you put
            that thing
            you wanted to
            bring along,
or reading,
            or thinking,
            or wondering.
Nothing mystical,
            though fakes
                        pretend.
Art is the everyday
            unfogging
            the mirror,
a service
            performed
by anyone
            who dares
            to see the need.

But language is
                        a mirror
            that tricks us.
On a journey
            of many turns,
                        a right
            can be wrong,
            and a left
                        can be right.
Yesterday Dick
asked me
            which letter
            was silent

in *scent*—
the *s* or the *c*?

What happens daily,
hourly,
minutely
(note the
shrinkage we arrive at
in that word)
is the mirror
the universe uses
to see itself.
Everything
a lesson.

Think of all
the things
you thought
would be fun
but weren't:
a dive into
a pile of leaves
(teaches
variance of densities
in matter,
but also
pain and
disappointment);
camping in the backyard;
a snowball fight
with older kids;
roadside attractions
with giant billboards
and nothing to offer
but plastic
souvenirs
to prove you stopped there.

But styles and
subject matters

change:
Mercedes
rhymes with Hades,
and future poets
may make much of that,
after
we've left them
walking
a parched earth
with daytime skies
that burn black.

Linguistically,
I prefer jungle
to rain forest.
People who talk
rainforests
are usually whining
about something;
jungle
smacks of adventure.

I claim no originality
for the experience
of the body,
which has felt nothing
billions
haven't felt before.
But what about
the mind?
Am I just a recycler
of old ideas,
worn-out wishes,
hopes,
dreams,
fears,
the latest runner
in a relay race
that started in the
dim pocket

of a cave
and crossed
every desert
across the millennia
to reach me?

What comes to us from
days of yore?
And what's
yore anyway?
A rarity,
a word of
singular meaning,
a latecomer
to the party of language,
coined
sometime after
nostalgic
sentimentality;
not just a past,
but a fabled past.
Yore
is the hunting ground
of our first stories,
history
filtered now
by distance
into
romantic
fictions.

But
pimpernels are
no longer heroic,
and adventure
today
is just a blunder into
misadventure,
an account

of surviving
one's mistakes.

This morning
a fog seeps through
the trees and
across
the open ground
behind the house
swallowing
everything
until it's all
I can see.
So let's hold steady
in the present:
Here's a question
on the internet:
Can you wear wingtips
to a funeral?
A fear of being
jaunty, I suppose.
So many layers
to the nonessential
in our world.
Peel back the onion
until you find
no onion there.

When I was Hamlet
half a century ago
the skull I held
in contemplation
was real,
shipped in from India
where human skulls
were marketed
at an affordable price,
and every night
before rehearsal,
I took it

from the prop room
and sat with it,
thinking —
not as Hamlet,
but as a college student
discovering
existentialism,
wondering
what real life history
had brought it to
my hands.
What man or woman's
mind
had been contained
therein,
and how far back?
A thousand years?
Or had we
walked the earth
in tandem,
two sides of the world,
one of us
living a life
that afforded time
to play
at being
someone else,
the other on a path
of anonymity,
graveless,
a lost
part of the whole,
now real in my hands,
each of us
without a true name
in the spotlight.

Want my take on the
spiritual?
No, of course not.

But don't think
of God
as a schoolmaster —
or anything
limited by
personality —
imagine a river;
believe
or don't believe,
there is still the river.

About prayer: well,
yes and no.
The river
won't change
it's course
for the asking,
but there's a current ,
invisible
and deep,
and it can take you
to a place you
want to go.

I would speak to
everything
because everything
listens.
Voice
is a disruption
of molecules
through air,
and hits
with its own certainty.
Like water
dripping
a hole through stone,
speak your violence
to the rock

until it splits.
Then go home calm.

But do it
in daytime.
The summer woods are
far too noisy
after dark.
Buzzing,
rasping,
croaking,
whirring,
plus cacophonies
of other sounds
that can't be spelled,
all of it
loud as a carnival,
all of it
an arm's reach
from where
you stand,
sounds of life,
clamoring,
relentless,
swallowing you up,
you're in it
but not of it,
a centerpiece only,
a statue
in the garden,
something
irrelevant,
oblivious
to what's really
going on.
Each woodland grove
conducts its business
without consideration
of your presence
or your thoughts.

If you want
to feel
unimportant
(and I
recommend it)
go stand in
the crowded
uncivilized
night
three hours after sundown
or three minutes
after a storm
and listen
in total ignorance
to an orchestration
beyond your
sense of
knowing.

If that brings sorrow,
so be it.
Sorrow makes us nobler
than the robot ant,
links us more
to pair-bond geese,
the dog,
the horse,
and others
capable of longing:
a word
more often felt
than said,
drapes our shoulders,
shifts our stare
downward,
turns a simple sigh
into a well
of loss.
Sorrow is a
starting point

for death
or resurrection,
the stage
preceding
hopelessness
or hope,
depending on
the wind,
the cold,
the rain,
and what you think of it.

Some say they see
faces
in the clouds;
I see faces
in shag carpeting,
flower beds,
linoleum,
tree bark,
any scarred
landscape
or unintended pattern
in paint
or rock,
or coat pile
on the bed.
Everything has a face
if you look
long enough
to see it.

Outside,
it's a perfect dawn:
lots of chirping,
the air
just cool enough
to feel brand new.
Above,
a pale blue sky

splashed with small,
misshapen
clouds,
and I approach
the vast brick building
without dread,
on time
for my appointment
with the specialist:
the sweeping
second hand
one way to
maintain a minor form
of order when
questions
urge chaos in the mind.

You know about
the universe,
appended by
the multiverse,
but on the page
there's only verse,
or sometimes
meta-verse,
a song about a song,
one thing
pretending
to be another,
a mirror for a mirror,
as I am prone
to demonstrate:

For mode,
I'll go with
Country-Western,
a quintessential form
for piling damage
upon damage:

A drunk sprawled
in the alley,
a ball cap on his head.
I asked him for
his problem,
but he sang
this song instead...

I'll skip the actual song
because we all
know where
it's going:
three plaintive verses
about loss
and longing
and who gets the blame.
Nothing about famine,
or pestilence,
or disease,
or what-not.
Country-Western
lives in
the trailer park.
and that's not me,
though twice I've
rented sadness there.

But I'm the kid who
jumped the fence
into East Germany
during the Cold War;
rode for a day
with Hell's Angels
up the California coast;
worked as
a bouncer in Manhattan,
derailed the Mob's
activities
in Alabama politics.
Time after time,

I've lived
crazed
by possibility and risk.

These days, I take
my vitamins,
and go
on pleasant walks.
I've learned that life
is the only thing
worth dying for.

In the parking lot
after the bone scan,
I notice buzzards
looping overhead.
Something
must be dead
beneath the canopy
of trees.
But I'm confident,
regardless.
Not everything's symbolic.

The definition
of *regardless,*
of course,
is ir*regardless.*
Think back:
Were you confused
when you
discovered that?

Discovery is the path
to creation
but it needs
an open mind.
If knowledge is
where we stop,
we'll never

know beyond
the known.
The next discovery
might knock
down the tower,
make us start
from scratch
(which ain't
so easy, bub —
accepted theories
are the hardest
things to kill).
Last year I hired
some men
to scrape
a place
in the side woods
for a garage,
and learned
we had
bad ground —
sand deposits
under eons
of vegetative rot.
They poured two feet
of gravel
against the likelihood
of sinking.
Now the car
is safe
from acorns,
and the birds
have nesting spots
to live
inside the storm.

At work
I have
administrators
running parts of

my life
who don't know
horses
can't be led
by pushing.

But I'm here now
on this page
someone has created
and you are, too,
and we're
thinking
now
together,
even across
the great gulf.
However you got here
thanks
for all the
patience
through this long haul
through unfamiliar
landscapes.

Is there some point,
some message
at the end
of the line?

On the whole,
maybe:
Get the mind
moving,
it can surprise you.

On the hole,
it's unfillable:
Knowledge is the
author
of uncertainty;

I didn’t know then
what I
don’t know now.

It’s Sunday,
early,
and the sun is bright,
but the slatted swing
in my backyard
hangs broken
by the late-night storm;
the iron chain
on
the left side lies
snake-like
on the ground.

This wasn’t from
some single
sudden
blustery blow:
for nine years now
the wind has
worked its way,
against the
wooden weight
to wear away the link
that held
the others
to the limb.
The break was
always
on its way,
the way
our
footsteps
grind us
bit by bit
until some
small

but crucial part
let's loose.

The swing itself
endures,
but since I've
grown too rickety
for climbs,
we'll give the thing
away,
and all will start again.
The white oak's limb
still holds
three
hundred
years
of sway.

For once
I'm caught up
on my work,
which leaves me free
to wander.
But that's a fallacy.
We're built
to move forward,
demanding purpose:
I think I'll move
sand
from the boys'
neglected sandbox
to the horseshoe pits.
We're selling
the house,
after all, so the place
needs to look lived in
but still fun.
That's not deceit:
we've liked it here,
amid acres of trees

and grass
and hillside.
Last evening the dog
worried
a vole
back and forth
in the gravel
outside
the garage,
then let it
scurry off
into the weeds
of the drainage ditch,
untouched.
The cat and I
both watched,
one of us enthralled
by nature
played as
just a game,
the other well-fed and
thus relatively
disinterested.

The thing about
being young:
you're stupid.
You understand little
but think otherwise.

The thing about
being middle aged:
you're worried—
the mortgage,
the job,
maybe college
for the kids,
religion
you have found
no use for,

the fragile politics
that hold the world
in place.
You think maybe hell
is the hand-basket
you're already in.
You think
you understand.

The thing about
being old:
one day
you wake up and
you're seventy, say,
and your spine
crunches
like celery
when you
turn your head,
and you can't
bend
far enough to
pick things off
the floor,
and your arteries
back up
like bad plumbing,
and your plumbing
goes bad, too,
and your
electrical system,
and probably
there's
some rot,
and new alarms will
send you monthly,
sometimes weekly,
to the doctor,
a teenage-looking
puppy,

proud and confident
        in that new
        white coat,
who thinks knowledge
means knowing,
        who offers options
like a waiter reeling off
                the specials
                of the day,
a waiter who doesn't
        know your tastes,
        your history
with other restaurants,
        or which new dish
                might kill you.
And every day thereafter
        you'll still
        wake up
in your seventies,
and it won't
        get
        any
        better,
and then you're in
                your eighties,
        your nineties,
        or god forbid
your hundreds—
        I've seen
        a few of those
and it's not pretty.

And yet.

        I like it here.
I finally have the room
to move around,
        even if stiffly.
        I get to
        stop and think.

Like now, for instance.
I understand
that understanding
has no bearing
on the hydrangea's
choice of color,
or on jewel beetles
boring
through tree bark,
devouring a meal
to make a home.

Know or don't know,
as you wish.
Understanding doing
does not affect
the need for doing.
Life is our
only real job,
and the purpose
of any job
is simply
to get on with it.

As time moves
across the surface
of a leaf,
it touches on eternal form,
where beauty (such
a loaded term)
and the leaf stands
for its
designated
moment
without decay.
What I mean is:
nature
opens up
a space
for every leaf to be

its capabilities;
but only once,
and briefly.
The peak
cannot be
balanced on.

Right now, looking out
my window,
I see trees,
spent rose bushes,
grass now
coming green
from winter dormancy,
some scattered stones.
Everything out there
is enough
in itself.
A rock is a rock,
no symbol attached.
But that's not how
things land
in poems,
that playground
of reflection,
where objects often
hint at pathways
somewhere else.
Which came first,
I wonder:
writing
or the hand-held mirror?
The mirror,
I suspect.
It goads us into
hoping
for something
after the fact,
something
more than the

perpetual loss
etched without ceasing
          into every surface
                    we see.

And why may we not
          choose the color
          of our hearse?
With lives of
infinite
          variation,
          must everything
default to black?
          We're born
to seek out color
across the
          visible spectrum—
          though
          immediately
I feel the weight
          of impossibility
          there:
          professionals
in the field
have racked up
          over 3,000
          registered colors,
and for some reason
          the count
                    continues.
          Go in any
          paint store
          and see the chaos
so many
          job-hungry
          fine-arts grads
                    have wrought:
forget blue,
forget red,
          there are

at least 47
tints and shades
of white:
polar mardi gras,
pre-dawn exultation
subdued jungle rain.
What the hell
are they
talking about?
Is our need
to evolve
so drenched
in desperation
that even color
has lost all
coherence?
I will not
paint my walls
avocado sunshine
or
moontide opalescence;
I'd sooner give in
to black—
which some claim
is no
color at all.

Speaking of which,
consider (again) God,
the great plurality,
too vast
for any
color wheel
of names:
let *All* stand in,
a proximate
shorthand
safeguarding
the process
so every bean

gets counted
into being.

Since change exists
(see:
cycles of growth,
decay,
evolution,
eruptions in the atom,
collisions
of galaxies,
shifts
in the unsteady
heart,
reversals
in the unsteady
mind,
or even an
always-well-meaning
brother-in-law
dying over breakfast
on the morning
of his anniversary;
he used to send me
books he thought
I might
take interest in
but which I
never read—
no time, no time,
though he took time
while having
even less).

There must have been
an imperfection
at the starting
point.

If All
were perfect
at inception
change of any kind
would
constitute corruption.

But problems
fuel our drive
toward harmony.
We smile
at passersby,
haul our garbage
to the curb,
feel guilty
for our trespasses.
We seek
forgiveness
from the All,
while All must find
salvation
on its own,
hoping
(I imagine)
toward
a universal sigh
that transforms
everything
it ever made
into an infinite and
eternal
Yes.

Meanwhile,
we live yin-yang,
see-sawing
between
blunders and apologies,
soaring high above
our pay grade.

We pass judgement
on the All:
Dinosaurs?
Bad idea,
so call them
fossil fuel
and try again.
Volcanoes?
Heavy-handed
at best.
And what's the deal
with those scorpions,
earthquakes,
childhood
diseases;
the Spanish inquisition,
Hitler,
clogged toilets,
pain,
confusion,
and a collective idiocy
that borders
on the unimaginable?

All
does the best
All can,
I suppose,
but fallibility exists.
Trial and error,
that's All there is.
On earth,
we
call it learning.

But let's be practical:
I can teach you
how to
wad a fitted sheet
(folding not

a realistic option),
          but the rest
you'll learn
          on your own.
We listen
          only to
          our own mistakes,
and even then
          not always.
We think in narrow
                    passages,
          alleyways
          slippery
with personal refuse,
          made comfortable
          only by habit;
rarely do we
think our way
          through eight-lane
          beltways
around the walled city
          of our misgivings,
                    gliding
          over the
          overpasses,
                    sliding
          under the
          underpasses,
taking the clearest
mental route
to really get somewhere,
to find our way
                    to some
          breakthrough
          in the mind
                    that feels
like coming home.

Today I took a walk
          around a pond

and saw an agitation
                        in the water.
            At first
I thought beaver,
            playing with
            a log,
both
            rolling
in the surface sun,
but as I watched
                        a wing
stretched out
then disappeared,
            then
            stretched
                        again,
and darker clarity
emerged.
            An alligator
            snapping turtle,
large
            and dangerous,
was taking down
                        a goose.
They whirled
            without ceasing,
            ripples
                        spreading
to the bank
beneath my feet,
            no splashing,
            just the slow
rolling of
two beaked bodies
                        locked,
            one full
            of airy grace,
one spiny
            and prehistoric.
Neither creature

made a sound.
I watched
for fifteen minutes,
then moved on.
The next day
there were
feathers
on the grassy slope.

Change is a balance:
better
for the turtle
equals
bad for the goose,
For every action
there's an equal
et cetera—
though that's not
always true
outside the laws
of physics:
some actions don't
pay off
the way the
mind anticipates.
I knew a man who
joined the Marines
but didn't
get brave.
I knew a woman who
became a nun
but didn't
cheer up any.

You want the
basic truth?
Your dog will die,
and you will grieve
the loss.
But keep moving:

the next slobbery,
clumsy,
big-footed pup
is waiting at the pound.

Existence,
you may have noticed,
is a
moving target,
unknowable,
unthinkable,
with no line drawn
between
fiber and stone.
Quartz crystal
takes in matter
and reconfigures it
to extend a
template of structure,
which is
what we do,
which is
what all
living things do.

Were minerals
the first life forms
to emerge
from the great vacuity?
Will they be the
final remnant
when all
that breathe
or circulate
are gone?

We value diamonds,
though they lack
the capabilities
of quartz.

But if we struck
the motherlode
and diamonds
were as plentiful
as sand,
their value would be
gone.
It's rarity that
props them up.
In exemplum:
on my walks I'd
rather spot a chipmunk
than a squirrel,
though the
squirrel has more
inherent majesty,
poised on its haunches
with its
bushy tail
arched high
for balance.
I'd rather spot a deer
than a chipmunk,
a snake
than a deer.
I'll say it
again:
it's rarity
that holds
our interest.
Remember that
when looking
in the mirror.
And don't look
too often.

Hot outside, mid-90s.
Back from a chore
to pick up bleach,
I caught a glint of light

wavering
            in the still air.
In the 12-foot gap
between the tow-trailer
            and garage
                        a spider
            had spun a web,
            three anchor lines
on each end
centering 57
            rings
precisely spaced,
            the gaps
            growing broader
            at the web's
                        outer reach.
It hung above the asphalt
            like a ghostly
            cross-section
            of a tree trunk.
In both cases
            the rings
            a measure of time.
The web wasn't there
            yesterday.
            I let it stand
                        for now.

What have I done since
            yesterday?

Our needs are clear:
            food, obviously,
            (with webwork
more of commerce
than of art)
            plus some measure
                        of safety
            from wolves
            and weather.

The rest is optional,
the catalogue of
wants
we push to such
extravagant extremes —
page after page
of feelings
and neuroses,
discomforts
to distract us
when the clatter
of the day
goes calm.
But
what I want
is what you want:
to dwell unafraid
in this half-dark;
to look hard
in the mirror
and see
some rough nugget
of worth.

But
I don't know,
says life.
What have you
done for me
lately?

Here's something
I notice
about hope:
it keeps odd hours,
coming
and
going
as it pleases,
like a

delinquent teen.
On the face of it,
I try to
be hopeful,
but then some sigh
escapes me,
and I have to
ask myself
where
this sudden
gust of disappointment
came from.

The mirror, maybe.
The world is full
of our reflections —
count the mirrors
in your home,
the mall,
the public restrooms.
The best
are at the carnival,
so blatant in
revealing our
distorted selves.

I have my own
arguments
with the mirror,
same as you.
Left side of my face
droops
a little,
which I'm not
crazy about —
a little trick my brain
played on me.
Now I look
slightly less

like myself,
but that's
everyone's
losing battle.

There are
two forms
of action:
the chemical
and the physical,
each
complementing
the other.

Explosions tell us
all we need
to know:
something
mixes
with something
and a massive
rejection
occurs,
each particle
so violated
it requires
escape.

Take fire:
the chemical
chain reaction,
we rely on to survive.
Its volatility
set everything in motion,
and here we are,
propelled
from an unknown
point of origin,
riding out the

expanding
debris field
of the Big Bang.

We're each a mirror,
a minor
reenactment
of reality's birth,
of change,
of growth,
of evolution,
an unending (
so far)
binary exchange.

I'm thinking now
that thinking
is an
intersection
of both sides:
An act of focus
coupled to
a concentrated
line of thought
that burns up calories
and tires a body out.
Thinking
is work
that creates work,
a chain reaction
in and of itself.
In that regard,
the universe
might be described
as a single mind
in action.

Let's call that
a beautiful notion.
But while there's

beauty in truth,
there's not much
truth in beauty,
which always
has an
expiration date.

You may have noticed
that I sometimes
circle back.
How can I not?
Like you,
I'm caught
between parallel
circuits
of atoms
and solar systems.
The earth itself
spins
without ceasing.
The wheel on asphalt
repeats itself
in one
identical turn
after another, but
without redundancy,
as the point
of contact
always changes;
stasis in
a state of progress.

When I was fifteen
the Beatles
sang about being
sixty-four,
old and gray,
in need of constant care.
Such decrepitude
seemed

unthinkable
to me then;
but the wheel turned,
and sure enough,
at sixty-four
my body tried to
shut me down.
I happened to survive,
and the wheel
turned
again.
Now sixty-four
is just another time
when I was young.

Archie once said
Hope's okay.
I think that's right —
less stringent than
religious faith,
no group-think grudge
if you reject it.
Both feed on
optimism,
clinging like kudzu.
Some argue faith
means more,
and I'd agree
that *faithless*
dooms our heartbeat
to a darkened room.
But *hopeless*
is as low
as we
can go.

Going to a better place:
a lot of life is
about moving,
and in fact I'm

        in that process
                now:
leaving one house
        for an older one
        that better suits
        our needs.
I could turn pro
at this point—
I've lived in
        18 houses,
        10 apartments,
        2 trailers,
        1 attic,
        1 basement,
        and
        1
        memorable stretch,
                of no address
                at all,
        just the nowhere of
                lower
                Manhattan.
Circumstance defines
        our level of
                acceptance
and home is what we
make the best of:
Here's a thing
        I know to be true:
        the warmth
        of a subway grate
        can feel better
        than a soft bed
                if there's
                no bed
        in the equation.

Today I reassembled
        a glass
        and steel

            desk
brought
from the previous house;
            49 of 55 pieces
            survived the trip,
but I made do,
            which is the way
            life works,
            and though
I'd walked by
            that desk
a thousand times,
            I had no clue
            how to
put it
                        back
                        together.
Had to do it
                        wrong
before I could
            do it right,
            which
once again binds me
            to the history
            of the world.
It's not
the opposable thumb
            that make us
            human,
it's our drive
to solve puzzles
            with it.

In many religions
            the afterlife
is about moving
            to the best
            neighborhood,
but here on earth

that can be
anywhere.

So can the worst,
and I've seen
some doozies,
but it's okay,
hopeless
can't move anywhere
but up.
Sitting
in a driving rain
with no dry place
to go,
one discovery
is that a downpour
can wash you
clean
even in the gutter.
Hold on to
your faith,
your hope —
whichever works better
in that hamster cage
of the mind:
The wheel
will turn
and turn again.
You're always headed
somewhere,
even when the vista
stays the same.

For this turn of the wheel
I bought
a fancy couch
and then a house
to put it in.
An upturn,
waiting

for the next
however
to set in.

Example:
I have a set of
bone china,
delicate and lacy,
I lug along
with every move,
a remnant of the
Lost City of Dresden.
My own father
was there
at the end,
the enemy in the sky.
Such hand-me-downs
I dare not
leave behind.

We learn from
everyone's
mistakes.
In my case
education
was a steady climb
toward uselessness:
geometry, dog
bless it,
taught me proofs,
and how to tile
my bathroom;
but then came trig,
where Mr. Gregor
made us memorize
the clotted squiggles
of the quadratic equation
without
revealing
why.

Maybe if he'd
staked it
to the ground,
I could have been
an architect
or engineer—
or whatever that thing
is used for—
out there building
bridges, maybe,
or
shaping monuments
that celebrate
our range of capabilities.
But anything
that starts with
minus B
plus or minus
the square root of...
is,
in my
narrow world,
without meaning.
Instead
I'm writing this.

So let's pick a word
at random
and see what
its geometry
might be:

bowls:
some bowls get used
once
and thrown away;
some bowls get left
on a shelf;
some bowls get filled
with nourishment

some bowls hold
  mysterious potions,
  sometimes deadly;
some bowls get broken;
some bowls get lost
  in the move;
some bowls never
  get washed;
some bowls last
  in memory;
some bowls
  are imaginary.

If all these bowls
    are bowls,
  there's no argument;
But say they're
  metaphors
for your most needful
  abstraction
  (love is
  one possibility,
  or
  fear,
  or
  devotion,
  or
  bitter resentment
  or
  endless longing
  or
  even hope,
    since it's
    always
    hanging
    around)
then
you might have some
  thinking
  to do.

But what difference
separates the
columned library
from its contents?
Both can
disappear
in conflagration —
i.e. the
Library of Alexandria,
that ancient
depository
of our knowledge.
Maybe it once held
the basic truth
of humankind.
Or maybe
our burning of it
tells us that anyway.

Today's escalation
of beauty vs. truth:
I walked into
a widow's web,
inducing panic,
I imagine,
in us both.
But once I'd cleared
the webbing
from my face and hair
and scrutinized
the spider
clinging
to the lintel
overhead,
I was impressed:
the rarest of its species,
a red widow,
more venomous
than a western rattler,
strikingly beautiful,

with sticklike
scarlet legs
angling from the
          bulbous
          opisthosoma,
its polka-dotted
markings,
          red and white
          on black,
unique
among its kind—
          especially here,
eight hundred miles
          from its
          Florida habitat.
Either the literature
          is wrong
or it hitched a ride
up north
with the people
          painting
          our house.
Of the five
North American widows,
          only the red
          injects a
          neurotoxin
from which
          the body can
never fully recover.

Let's think
          of something else.

I see a bird
          fly past my window,
                    and think of
                    how they
          surf the wind like
we would water,

though
we can't plummet
to the ocean floor
the way a bird
can drop
from
the sky.

That's my presumption,
anyway:
I've never
seen one fall
from flight
or even from a limb.
I've never seen one die,
except by
intervention:
a shotgun blast,
a cat,
a plate-glass
window,
or even by a larger bird.
Where do they all go
to die?
That's one small pebble
on the mountain
of things I don't
undestand.
But
it's okay,
I think,
not to understand—
if I understand
the word—
because
to understand
is to
stand
under;
to be a logical pillar

of support.
It stands
to reason, then:
the more
I understand,
the greater the weight
of what the mind
must bear.
Sure, too little
understanding
and we might
wade into quicksand
just to see what
we'll become;
but too much
understanding
and the brain
might buckle.
Maybe, then, there's
more to
fret about
than knowledge of
good and evil;
there's also knowledge
of the trivial,
the mundane,
the self-evident,
the irrelevant,
the useless,
the useful,
the arts,
the sciences,
and whatever
other avenues
absorb our time
without a payback
of enlightenment.

But I don't know.

A black squirrel
down the lane
fell from a tree
yesterday,
but shook it off
and re-climbed.
Squirrelly.
They're dancing
all over
the yard
these days —
the coming season
spurs them
with its frantic drives.
They leap for
untried branches,
the way
all lovers do;
the way
all artists do.

The younger dog
hungers for it —
launching through
the moment
of the
open door.
Years now,
and she's
caught nothing,
but chase alone
still keeps her
hopes alive.

Lessons
everywhere we
look:
from spider,
from squirrel
from dog,

even from the act
of looking.
We speculate
toward understanding
in the chaos
of a cloudless day.

Knowing is a goal,
I guess,
but knowledge
needs assumptions
for support,
so where does that
leave us?
Sometimes
what's obvious
is unreliable:
that twig
is an insect
made to fool the eye,
that spread
of dead leaves
obscures a copperhead
from your
next footfall.
Don't trust the first
unguarded glance,
is what I'm saying.
Save believing
as the only
option left.

Like now:
outside
the east window
a cardinal
flies back and forth
between an
empty nest
and the rest of

what it knows.
        My hope is that
        it's scouting a spot
for the next brood,
but it might just be
        locked
        in a cycle of
confusion
and mourning
                for eggs
                or chicks
                that
        disappeared.
Two options, and
        my hope can't
        tip the scales
        to bring about
                belief.
No creature's heart
        beats loud enough
        for nature
                to be moved.

Sure, I can be
        pessimistic
        about the
direction
of our footprints:
        Beneath
                a big sky
        flocked
        with stars,
        bequeath
                a pig sty
        pocked
        with scars.

There is, of course
        a snake
        inside the garden;

many, probably,
though they
don't emerge
in knots.
I spent some time
with one
the other day—
a slim four-footer
sunning itself
across the roots
of a tree
in the side yard.
I moved in close;
it paid me
great attention,
head raised,
body loaded
like a spring in twenty
almost imperceptible
crooks,
but never sprang
for cover
or defense.
Maybe it sensed
my only driving force
was curiosity.
At first I took it for
a rat snake,
so sleek and black
it was,
but crouching near
I saw a
dark brown stripe
along its
left side,
(mirrored, I presume
by another
on its right,
so fond is
nature

of its symmetry)
an unrecorded variation
in the species —
the gap
between what's real
and what we know.

And still, we all persist
in making lists
to organize
a structure of beliefs.

And listing now,
starboard,
belief
is all I need to
see the station
up ahead.
It's time
to turn my focus
to an exit,
dear passengers
of the jury,
(as we all are,
daily).
As long as we're
alive,
our headlong
rush
toward certainty
never ends,
but life
is not a book,
not a poem.
In truth,
the outside
flutter
of the searching bird
is what we're
here for:

the gasp of air,
the strain
of movement,
the angle of light
stabbing the eyes
into tears,
the noise
all around us,
first a mysterious jumble,
then
brick
by
brick,
communication,
and the dazzling,
dumbfounding
recognition
that
even when the sun
goes down,
and the eye
sees nothing
in the shadow,
we are
part of something,
not
stranded here
alone.

Look, I know
we all have
guesses,
and there's room for
every theory
to be right.
If the universe is infinite,
then every
finite thing
contained

therein
must,
by comparison,
be infinitely small.
Not just
the subatomic
but you and me,
and the planet
we stand on,
the solar system
we employ
to measure years,
the galaxy
spiraling
out around us,
and the rest of it
(whatever
it may be).
Otherwise,
(a confident word
for emphasizing
truth)
somewhere out there
a border
marks
the end of things,
and if we travelled
there
we'd find a moment
of transition,
a littoral zone
between what is
and isn't;
between everything
and nothing
known and unknown;
knowable and
unknowable;
us,

and existence
    without
    us.

When I started
    all this,
    my desk was one
I'd worked at
twenty years,
    and it was
    old already
    when it came to me.
Last week we moved
    and the desk
was too beat up
to make the trip.
    The people
at the Goodwill store
    refused it,
so I broke it into
    seven pieces
    and hauled it
    to the dump.
For an interim
    I dragged a
    hard chair in
from the dining room,
and worked
    at an old fold-up
frozen-dinner table.
Now, my new desk,
    bought cheap
    at Hope Thrift
    (how perfectly
    appropriate)
on Patterson Avenue
    isn't new,
but it's only four pieces
and easy to

put together.
The new house
isn't new
either,
but thirty-three
years old,
same as Jesus,
though not nearly
as forgiving.
I couldn't begin
to count the pieces,
but a lot of them
need work.

The room I'm in
has empty walls
and a hard floor
so as I read this
aloud
my voice
echoes,
which is another kind
of mirror.

Can you see an
allegory
in all this?
If so,
I'd like to hear from you.
And
if
as you read this,
I've reached already
the reaper's
cutting edge
and so
been rendered
speechless,
I'd like to
hear from you

                        anyway.
You never know.

In dreams I know
how to behave,
            how to pick
            the intricate locks.
We all do,
            one way or another.
The challenge
            is to carry back
            our lessons
to the waking world.
            Dog, god,
            mirror facing mirror
            for an act of
                        infinite reflection:
every moment
            offers a stray thread
                        to pull;
realize that,
            and
                        unstitch
            the fabric
            of the universe.

An apple falls
            on Newton's head
            and he tracks
the moment
                        into Law.
Robert the Bruce
            watches a spider
            in a cave
and learns to
                        persevere.
            Everything is an
                        example of
something
            beyond itself.

Every object
is born of action,
every action
has a source,
and every source
has a source
of it's own,
and so does that one,
and that one,
and on and on,
down
and
down
until every source
converges
in a common start,
the one
that brought
time into being
and us
into thinking;
that
singular
seminal
moment
of everything expanding,
exploring
a way forward
from the first
startled
beat
of the universal heart.

Every beginning
is also
an end,
and every end is
an experience—
except maybe

the last one.
When the
condemned
approaches
the chopping block,
which
matters
more
in the final focus
of the mind:
the executioner
or the axe?

The executioner,
I'd imagine;
there's nothing
to hope for
from the axe.

What's known
to every tramp
with a bundle
on a stick:

starting anywhere,
you can go
anywhere.

If answers are the core
of your desires,
pick anything and
go from there:
that shiny rock
in the gravel,
that earthy scent
winding its current
on the breeze,
that birdsong
trilling in a distant
piney grove;

whatever the light
                    illumines
or the dark
                    overtakes,
          engage with it,
                    until
it makes
          the sense
                    you need.
And never
          underestimate
          an afterthought;
it might pull up
          a puzzle piece
          that fits.
Then call it a day.
Call it contentment.
Call it the part
          becoming equal
          to
          the whole.
Call it a
          unified theory
          of everything.

Outside, the day's
          heat,
          which topped
          a hundred
in mid-afternoon,
          has broken
in the gloaming,
and cicadas
          are chorusing
          their usual song
          toward dark.
I've never minded
hot days,
the way they
          cloak me

        so completely
as I pass through
        the doorway,
a statement from
the world
        that it is there
        and I am in it.

Meantime,
        (which is the
        only time)
I find myself
awash in gratitude:
                for the dirt
                and waters
        and their
        casual support
(though ultimate
        disinterest)
        in my being;
for the blood and air,
                circulating
                through me
in such helpful ways;
        for the
                outward sky
        that refills daily
                with our
        mysteries;
        for the dog
that cocks its head
                in curiosity;
        for the words
that sometimes
come out right;
        for the people
        who gave me
all the
        good and grave

examples
I required,

and at this moment,
for you,
in particular,
for coming along —
to whatever degree
that's true —
so generous
with your time,
even though this was
not
your trip to write.
But
that's a false
distinction,
a superficial wrinkle
in our
circumstance.
It's my belief
we carry the same
leaky basket
up the hill,
we push the same
leaky rowboat
from the shore,
we suffer the same
leaky longings
for a way
across
the desert,
a passage
through the mountains,
a detour
around the swamp.
We're each
the mirror
of all selves.

Everything here belongs
to you
as much as me.
We earned our passports
with that first
halting intake
of breath.
Forget the illusion
that I got here first,
forget that I called dibs.
Volcano your
momentum
toward the
speed of light,
and dream
something
big
to wake up to.

Acknowledgments

Portions of this book appeared in *The Poetry Miscellany,* edited by Rick Jackson, and in *Hamilton Stone Review,* edited by Kevin Stein.

My thanks to the League of Extraordinary Gentlemen: David Wojahn, Thom Didato, Kent Ippolito, John Ulmschneider, and Harrison Candelaria Fletcher, for the weird reads and all the strange music that followed.

My thanks also to the usual suspects: Curt Musselman & Cecelia Brown, Jim Frazee, John Rice, Dave Pickering, Sam Teeter, Pete Hull, Mitch Snead, Neal Kassman, Dick Boaz, and the Gibbon brothers, all of whom have granted me regular reasons for getting me out of my head to discover a new course.

And to Kevin Morgan Watson for his dedication to keeping art alive.

Clint McCown has published six previous collections of poems, four novels, a collection of short fiction, a collection of essays, and a craft book on writing fiction. His poems, fiction, and essays have appeared in more than ninety-five national magazines and journals. He is the only two-time winner of the American Fiction Prize. Additionally, his work has been honored with the Midwest Book Award, the Society of Midland Authors Award, the Gable Prize from Graywolf Press, the Germain Breé Book Award, three Notable Essay citations in the Best American Essays series, an NEA grant, more than forty Pushcart nominations, and the Associated Press Award for Documentary Excellence for his investigations of organized crime and political corruption. He received theatre training at the Circle-in-the-Square on Broadway and is a former principal actor with the National Shakespeare Company and the Puerto Rican Traveling Theatre. Several of his plays have been produced, and he has worked as a screenwriter for Warner Bros. and as a creative consultant for HBO Television. He is a former editor of Indiana Review and was the founder of the Beloit Fiction Journal, which he edited for twenty years; for four years he served as General Editor for the AWP Intro Journals Awards. He is a professor emeritus in the graduate writing program at Virginia Commonwealth University and for twenty years he served as a member of the writing faculty for the Vermont College of Fine Arts low-residency MFA program. In 2021 he was inducted into the Writers Hall of Fame at Wake Forest University.

www.ingramcontent.com/pod-product-compliance
Lightning Source LLC
LaVergne TN
LVHW091133080826
845145LV00008B/2134

* 9 7 8 1 9 6 8 7 8 3 0 3 7 *